"The depiction of Gomati reveals the despair of our countless marginalized women, their courage, their paradoxes, their culpability, and their condition. Who will change their fate? When?"

Gopal Krishna Gandhi
AMBASSADOR OF INDIA IN NORWAY

"I must say that it is very strong and powerful, and of course, very grim… it is an excellent parable for human dignity and becomes almost an epic in its dimensions…"

Shyam Benegal
NOTED FILMMAKER

"Gomti's sufferings and indomitable will to save her soul and defy all oppressions are a message of hope."

Dr Birendra Kumar Bhattacharya
FAMOUS ASSAMESE WRITER
JNANPITH AWARD WINNER

EMBERS IN SNOW

Translated by Indira Mittal

Himanshu Joshi

ISBN: 978-93-56822-15-3
eISBN: 978-93-56822-16-0

Prabhakar Prakashan (P) Ltd.
Plot No.-55, Main Mother Dairy Road
Pandav Nagar, East Delhi-110092
Phone: 011-40395855
WhatsApp: +91 9319228272
E-mail: sales@pharosbooks.in
Website: www.prabhakarprakashan.com
First Edition: 2023

EMBERS IN SNOW
By Himanshu Joshi

Publisher's Note

In this distinguished translation of a literary masterpiece by Himanshu Joshi (1935-2018), we are thrilled to present a profound exploration of the human experience. As a renowned author and social commentator, Joshi has left an indelible mark on Hindi literature, captivating readers with his insightful narratives and unwavering commitment to addressing social injustice.

Within the pages of this translated novel, you will be transported to a world where human emotions unravel and societal inequalities are exposed. Joshi's eloquent prose, skillfully rendered in this translation, captures the essence of joy, sorrow, love, and resilience with remarkable clarity. Prepare to embark on an extraordinary journey, where the complexities of the human heart are laid bare.

Joshi's storytelling prowess extends far beyond the realm of mere entertainment. With a keen eye for social dynamics, he fearlessly confronts the prevailing injustices of our time. Through his vivid portrayal of characters and their struggles, he casts a piercing light on issues such as caste discrimination, gender bias, and economic disparity. In doing so, he challenges readers to reexamine their own beliefs and compels us to confront the inherent inequities that persist in our society.

As you delve into the translated pages of this novel, you will encounter characters who become companions on your literary voyage—flawed yet relatable, resilient yet vulnerable. Their stories will stir your emotions, provoke introspection, and ignite a desire for change. It is through their experiences that Joshi shines a light on the shared humanity that binds us all together.

From the backdrop of village life to the complexities of urban existence, from the struggles of everyday life to the intricacies of politics and politicians, the world of Himanshu Joshi's story expands gradually, encompassing various aspects of the human experience. However, Joshi never forgets that the essence of literature is life itself, and the purpose of literature is to inspire us to live, not die. The author's inherent inclination is to raise his voice against the exploitation of human beings at any level.

The novel 'Kagaar Ki Aag' in Hindi was published in its entirety on January 4, 1976, in the silver jubilee issue of 'Saptahik Hindustan.' Its publication brought to light the author's vision of understanding the status of women in society, highlighting the exploitation they face due to their vulnerability. The novel challenges the notion that women must remain helpless and perpetually subjected to exploitation. The author believes that every individual must find strength within themselves to escape from exploitation.

The popularity of this novel is evident through its numerous editions and the affection it received from readers. After its publication in 'Saptahik Hindustan,' countless letters poured in from readers, including well-known writers. Yashpal, a distinguished storyteller of that time, wrote a letter praising the powerful depiction of mountainous life in the novel. He wrote, "The novel portrays a powerful depiction of mountainous life. I have witnessed this mountainous region up close on several occasions. The memories of the past came alive after reading it. The everyday life of almost all our mountainous regions is like this—filled with struggles."

Not only in India but scholars from abroad were also captivated by the story of this novel. Professor Liu Guo Nan, a Hindi professor at Peking University in China, expressed his admiration in a letter to the author. He shared his personal connection to the story, revealing that the protagonist Gomti reminded him of his own niece who faced similar hardships in China. He requested permission to translate the novel into Chinese. He wrote—

> "To tell you the truth, you have written it so well that I read it in one breath. I liked it very much. Maybe because its story is my own family's story. In China, before the 'Freedom Movement,' I had a niece. She was beautiful and energetic. She used to call me 'Mama Ji.' Although she was two or three years older than me. In childhood, she used to come to our house, and we used to play together. I would always lag behind her in running, climbing trees, and catching fish. But poor thing, she was born into a poor family. Her father was a labourer in the fields, and her mother worked in the landlord's house. Our house was so poor that we couldn't even help them even if we wanted to. One day, her marriage suddenly took place. She bid farewell, crying. It turned out that her husband was completely blind. At that time, my niece was only fourteen years old. Many times, she ran away from home. But every time she was caught and beaten badly. Still, she never gave up. Her courage never broke. Finally, one day, she succeeded in running away. Where did she go, no one knew. Neither my parents nor my sisters wanted to know about her. No one asked anyone about this relationship. Because a woman leaving in this way was considered a stain for parents and relatives…
>
> After independence, I joined a land improvement team and went to the neighbouring district. There I found out that my beloved niece had lost her life while struggling with a landlord. Reading your novel, I kept realizing that its protagonist Gomti is none other than my deceased niece. She is still alive today, holding her child's hand in the vast land of India, wandering in the darkness, I don't know where she is going. It's already morning in China, but poor thing, she doesn't know how she ended up wandering in India!"

While reading this story, one becomes fully immersed, feeling its truth in every fiber. The author acknowledges that the story of Gomti is not an exact account of real events, as its sheer magnitude would be hard to believe. To maintain authenticity while avoiding disbelief, the author consciously toned down certain aspects of the suffering portrayed. This approach creates a taut narrative, where tension and intensity increase as Gomti, the central character, progresses in her pivotal role. The novel hints at the arrival of a metaphorical morning, symbolizing hope and change, while emphasizing that escaping oppressive circumstances requires taking the first step and transcending weakness.

The story primarily revolves around Gomti, who is relentlessly pursued and mistreated due to her youth, beauty, femininity, poverty, and helplessness. Despite the cruelty she endures, Gomti displays tremendous endurance, sacrifice, and will to survive, becoming a beacon of hope for the oppressed and the downtrodden worldwide.

The novel which was written originally in Hindi has already been translated into Chinese, Norweigian, Nepalese, Burmese, Tamil, Malayalam, Punjabi, Dogri, Marathi, Konkani, and Oriya. The translation of "Kagaar Ki Aag" was praised in several languages, including the Konkani translation by Sahitya Akademi Award Winner Chandrakant Keni and the Odia translation by Jnanpith Award Winner Dr. Pratibha Ray. The theatrical performances of the novel left the audience deeply moved, as vivid portrayals of characters like Gomti, Pirma, and Kunnu shed light on the struggles of marginalized society. The story transcended boundaries of nation, time, and circumstance, becoming everyone's story and resonating with people from all walks of life.

For this present translation, we extend our deepest gratitude to the translator, whose dedication and skill have brought this masterpiece to life for a wider audience. Through their remarkable ability to capture the nuance and essence of Joshi's writing, they have preserved the integrity and power of the original work, allowing readers to immerse themselves in this thought-provoking narrative.

Dear reader, we invite you to embark on this literary journey—a journey that transcends borders and languages. Through the translation of this novel, we hope to bridge the gap between cultures, fostering understanding and empathy. Let the words of Himanshu Joshi resonate within you, inspiring you to contemplate the human condition and to actively participate in creating a more just and compassionate world.

We are honoured to present this translated edition of Himanshu Joshi's novel, and we hope that it will captivate your heart, challenge your perspectives, and leave an indelible imprint on your literary soul.

Prabhakar Prakashan

Delhi, India-110092

PREFACE

This is the story of a village. Any name can be given to the village, characters can also be called by any names, it does not make any difference. This is the life story of those poor people, who are outcasted and neglected for centuries.

Truly speaking, they are the living images of misery, sorrow incarnate, and the embodiment of pain. Gomti, Pirma and Khimu-Ka are the black and white sketches of agony, drawn by the hands of time.

Old Khimu-Ka is still alive, a witness to this tragic story. He looks at a tiny patch of barren land and says, 'Yes, this is, where the broken hut was. Both brothers used to live here! The elder's name was Pirma and the younger...' He cannot say anything more and just gazes strangely into the void. This patch of land now is full of tall wild grass and thorny bushes of 'Sisuna'. A delicate plant of 'Fanyia' is peeping from across the mud wall. Even today the bellows are at work—cold iron is heated. The hammering by cold iron on hot iron, goes on and dazzling sparks of molten iron fly around in the dark.

Whenever a human shadow is seen, far away in the depth of darkness, people hide behind closed doors in sheer terror.

I have not written the true story of Gomti in all its realities. If I had written the whole truth, people would not believe that it is really true. I confess, I had to minimise the endless miseries of her life in my narration, so that the true story may not look like untruth.

Where is Gomu now?

What happened to Kunnu?

I do not know myself. I did go to that village, a few days ago where Gomti used to live. Her old mother had died recently. I made enquiries in the village but could not get any information. However, some of the literate villagers were upset with me for publishing the personal life of their own village. Why did I write about it in the papers? Why did I throw mud on Gomti's character?

How could I commit the folly of casting aspersion on her character? She was more pious than any Sati Savitri.

When this novel was serialised in 'Saptahik Hindustan' by the name 'Kagaar ki Aag' I got a tremendous response from my readers through a vast number of letters. I cannot still follow how this simple tale of a neglected remote village could touch the readers so deeply. This is another big surprise for me after the publication of my previous novel 'Chhaya Mat Chhuna Man'.

I consider myself very lucky that not only the common readers liked this story, even the intellectuals appreciated it I am sure the amount of response I got from my readers can make any author feel proud.

Literature is not merely an entertainment, it is a higher mission for me. I have made all efforts to render voice to the common man, crushed by innumerable miseries. I am unable to separate my agony from theirs. Hence, I have tried to talk of my own pain through their medium.

If the agony of these helpless people will compel you to think about them, I will feel my effort has not been wasted.

HIMANSHU JOSHI

7/C-2, Hindustan Times Apartments,
Mayur Vihar, Phase-I,
Delhi-110091.

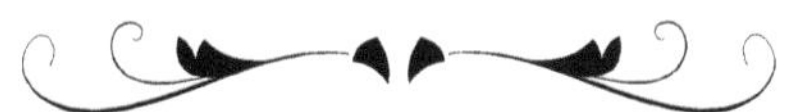

EMBERS IN SNOW

ONE

It had happened twice before.

This time again, she had fled alone under the dark.

Her mother was distressed.

"Why have you come like this, Gomu, all alone?"

The dry parched lips and the cobweb wrinkles spoke of a lifetime of sorrow and fear, "Who'd want to accompany a wretch like me, Ija[1]? Even death evades me." Covering her face with her palms, rough as the oak bark, Gomti wept like a little girl.

Her mother argued with her.

"Woman has only one home, Gomu. You have to spend your whole life there. Times change. Try and bear with it a little..."

"But how long, Ija?" Gomti pulled up her grimy, tattered kurti[2], "look at this, see for yourself."

"So you still want to say something?"

"Why did not you kill me at birth, Ija?"

The old woman shuddered and closed her eyes. Gomti's slender body was bruised all over. Gathering her tears in her tattered chaddar she wailed.

---

1. 'Ija' - Mother
2. 'Kurti' - Long skirt

"Ill-fated wretch! Those demons will tear you to pieces and devour you..."

The mother tried to reason with her daughter. But no reason could reach Gomti's disturbed mind.

Her uncle-in-law had beaten her with a thornbrush stick right in front of her husband Pirma. Her aunt-in-law had also pounced upon her like a hawk, pulling her hair. "You shameless harlot, reared on crumbs, why did you come to us, you beggar? Wasn't one husband enough for your blood thrust? Godali was saying that she saw you eating 'jalebis'. Where did you go with the forest guard yesterday? Why were you talking to the animal doctor? Out to sully our reputation, eh you? Going wild with eaddies, trollop?"

Gomti had borne the kicks and blows in silence. If Dharamram 'sarpanch' had not turned up on his round of the village, they would have killed her. He had intervened and freed her; somehow. Pirma had watched dumbly, huddled in a corner. Seeing his mother beaten so mercilessly, little Kunnu had crouched near the wall, numb with fear, not daring to cry, so terrified was he. Later Gomti had gathered him to her breast and had lain sobbing in the small hut, thatched thinly with old straw.

Pirma had lain nearby, coughing all night.

Whom could she tell? Who would believe her that she went to the animal doctor for medicine for her husband? There was nothing more than that between them. As for the forest guard, she had not seen him for a whole week. She went to the jungle in the company of the village women to cut grass, and returned also along with them. Where could Godali see her? And when?

The shameless hussy herself was in the habit of asking the forest guard for a 'bidi' often and when Godali had emerged from the log cabin built in the forest for storing resin, her skirt was spotted wet...

Gomti had not uttered a word despite having seen everything with her own eyes. Fearing that Gomti might talk about her, the cunning Godali had tried to forestall it by making false allegations against her.

But what had better these cursed villains? Her uncle-in-law's frightening face loomed large before Gomti's eyes... drunken, red-eyed, bushy moustache...

"Your Kaka's intentions are not honest. His mind is evil. He casts lustful glances at me..." As always, Pirma had snubbed her.

"Are you out of your mind, suspecting an old man? It is sinful. You will suffer for it in the next birth. If the people hear this, what will they say? They will spit at us...and all this for nothing."

Gomti had given up. Pirma was weak in the head, ignorant of the wily world, a dumb and docile animal and everyone knew it. His uncle had driven him like an ox all his life. As long as the family was one, he had never been fed properly; dried left-overs were thrown casually into his broken plate and, his cousin Tejuva's discarded clothes were given for him to wear.

For the past few days, the old man had gone mad. He would send Pirma to keep watch over the potato fields. The unfortunate wretch spent the whole night driving away porcupines with cries of, "Qa—lo—lo—lo—! Chhepo! Chhepo! H-a-a-t—Chha! H-a-a-t—Chha!" A wink of sleep, and the whole field would be ravaged. When all slept and the whole village was deserted like the cremation ground, the lecherous old uncle-in-law would tiptoe in the dark to her crumbling hut and his fingers went for the flimsy door flaps. She had chased him away two or three times, but he had not given up. He returned snivelling...

Last night he had managed to open the flaps. Gomti had not known what to do. Pulling out the sickle she always kept beneath her pillow, she had aimed it in the dark, and only then had the shameless lecher slunk away, like a beaten dog with its tail between its legs. In the morning there had been queries, "How did you get hurt on your forehead, Kaliya?" Pirma's uncle had hedged.

"Slipped in the dark, yaar. Can't see clearly now after nightfall..."

But he had been waiting to take his revenge alright, and took it yesterday. His wife had conspired with him, and Godali had been bribed with some jaggery. The whole plot had been hatched...

Gomti's mother helped her to lie down near the fire and began applying warmed pads to her sore welts.

There was nothing to eat in the house. Spreading some hot ash on the hot plate she roasted some soybean which they both munched, and washed it down their throat with plenty of cold water which also stilled the remaining pangs of hunger. Then both fell asleep.

Her mother was now too old to work at all, and it was becoming more and more difficult to earn even two meals a day. She went hungry for days, for her a month now had many ekadashi[3].

Gomti lay swaddled in rags near the dying fire. Sleep deserted her and she wondered what hour of the night it was. She had no refuge in this wide world. Her husband was demented. No father-in-law or mother-in-law. There was only her husband's younger brother serving in the

---

3. 'Ekadashi' - Day of fasting after every full moon.

army, posted somewhere at the front. Gomti had no other kith or kin besides her old mother and she too with her feet in the grave.

Gomti had contemplated suicide many a time. She needed only to hang herself from the tallest of the mountain trees, the 'dulla' tree, and it would rid her of a life of misery. But little Kunnu's innocent face would appear before her eyes, stamping out the gruesome thoughts from her mind. The small hands.. .the tiny milk teeth...She would feel him in the dark...Pirma's hands like blackened stumps would tug at her tattered 'pallu'[4]...

She knew what Kaliya wanted... That Gomti should elope with someone, or drown in the nearest river and Pirma should serve him all his life, like a slave. After Pirma's death, he could claim the land as his, being Pirma's kith and kin. The three well-irrigated fertile fields in Gajaar, ideal for paddy cultivation, were already mortgaged to him for rupees three times twenty, borrowed at the time of Pirma's mother's cremation. There was still more land to be grabbed...

Only the other day Tejuva had boasted at one of the shops in Pokhari, "If mad Pirma dies, I will keep Gomti for myself..."

Gomti's face had become her misfortune. If only she could claw it ugly, or singe it with the torch of the deodar (cedar) bark. God was cruel to have given her such beauty only to make her suffer for it. Her own relatives were her enemies...

Her mother turned in sleep.

"Still awake Gomu?"

"I can't sleep, Ija." Gomti was distracted with worry.

---

4. 'Pallu' - End of a wrap

"Have you people ever heard from Debiya, thy brother-in-law?"

"Not for quite some time now. There was a letter around the month of magh-phalgun[5]. Tuliya was telling us that he has been posted elsewhere. There has been no letter since then."

"Then he could not have sent you people any money either."

"No. He used to send us something every two or three months for us to survive on but even that is not coming now. These foes of ours are after our lives. Who knows whether they might have written something to him...?"

Gomti fell silent. The dark night was still. Something came to her mind.

"Any news of elder Kaka's daughter, Ija?"

"Not yet..." Gomti's mother seemed reluctant to answer, "there are rumours that she has started living with a barber in Tanakpur."

Elder Kaka's daughter Dhari and Gomti had been close friends. They had gone together to the Devidhura[6] fair once and had sung the mountain lores all night, swaying to the rhythm of the hudka[7].

Where had those days gone?

Gomti sat with her chin on her knees, having strayed far in thoughts...

---

5. 'Magh-Phalgun' - months of February-March
6. 'Devidhura' - A holy shrine
7. 'Hudka' - A percussion instrument, quite like Lord Shiva's 'damroo'

TWO

The tempting aroma of freshly baked, thick 'rotis' of black 'manduva'[8] flour... A patch of cool sunshine outside the thinly thatched hut... The cawing of the crow perched on the pomegranate tree... Gomti gazed at it. Her mother was awake, baking thick black 'rotis'... "Where did the flour come from, Ija?" Gomti could not help asking.

"I borrowed it. You have not eaten anything since yesterday."

There were only four 'rotis'. Three thick ones, one very small. Her mother put three before Gomti, and started chewing the fourth herself, working her jaws as though chewing a piece of leather. She put some salt ground with green chillies on a leaf, and pushed it towards Gomti.

"So much? I will not be able to finish all this, Ija."

"Hai! Starving since yesterday, and she says she cannot eat even these two 'rotis', the size of ear lobes?" Gomti did not argue any more. Picking up the 'rotis' she began swallowing morsels with the salt.

"Why did you not bring Kunnu with you?"

"How could I? How would I get him to cross the river? I had come to the woods to cut grass, and from there I ran here."

---

8. 'Manduva' - The coarsest and cheapest of foodgrains, rather like finger millet flour.

"Is there anything to eat in thy house, Iju[9]?" Gomti's mother asked.

"Where from? Whatever was grown in the fields we used for meals. These days we labour in others' fields and earn barely enough to feed ourselves; hardly two 'rotis' in the evening after a whole day of bone-crushing labour. If only Kunnu's father would work, we would not be facing such hardship. I used to hope that one day we too would set up a smithy, and get some iron on loan from places like Khetikhan or Dhunaghat. If we could make even one or two pots and pans, we would earn something for meals at least. God knows What sorcery they have worked on Kunnu's father. He does whatever they tell him to do. These days he is being sent out to guard the potato fields. With only a torn blanket for cover, he is drenched in the rain all night. For all I know he might be found dead in the fields one day. If he does not die this way, these demons will poison him to death with 'dhatoora'[10]. As it is, his bones are jutting out from smoking so much 'ganja'[11]." Gomti could not go on, the morsels seemed to choke her. She put aside the piece of black 'roti'.

"My Kunnu will not have eaten for two days now..." Gomti was torn with anxiety.

Mother and daughter spread a torn mat in the inner courtyard to sit and bask in the sunshine. There was not much of it, anyway, the fleecy black clouds spreading out to devour most of it. Gomti sat quiet, picking her teeth.

---

9 'Iju' - Daughter

10. 'Dhatoora' - Poisonous wild plant, intoxicant in light doses.

11. 'Ganja' - Pot

Her mother's head lay on her knees as she picked lice. The white hair was matted grey with grime. Gomti wondered how long it had been since it had been washed.

"I have not many years to live, Gomti," her mother muttered, lost in thought, "I wanted so much to see you happily settled before dying, it is my last wish... These remaining patches of land would be yours but the village-head Harkishan had got the deed changed in his name during your father's lifetime. This I have learnt only now. The household utensils were taken as interest, your father was made to plough his fields without any wages; and now when my end is near I have been cheated so wickedly. Such a base deed, and he a 'brahmin'?" Gomti's mother sighed heavily.

"And if I were to get these fields what would I do with them." Gomti thought aloud. "Who would come this far to till the land? Kunnu's father is not the kind. If only he would go to saw wood, or collect resin, if only he would dig in the quarries and supply the stones to house builders, we could get by. But his ways are queer; he sits quiet, as if turned to stone... I do not like to stay in the village any more. I will fling aside everything one day and go my way. Do not blame me then..."

"Quiet, quiet you, foul mouth! One does not talk like this. What will the folk say? Suffer your fate. Die if you want to. That is the only salvation for you..."

Gomti's hands were still. She stared away into the sky. Her mother went on muttering.

"Go home this time, Iju. If they beat you another time, come away then, never to return. I will not insist... We have to think of the people. All will curse your father. His soul in heaven will be unhappy."

"Is there any happiness left for us in this hell, Ija?" Gomti wanted to ask.

By late noon the news had spread in the entire village that Gomti was of loose character...that she had sought shelter in her mother's house... If she was good, would she have left her husband's house?... She was carrying on numerous affairs, that is why her uncle-in-law had thrashed her...

If there were tale carriers, there were many who sympathised with her, too.

"Born to a sad fate, poor girl." Some women whispered, "Barely two or three years old she was when her father passed away. Widowed at the tender age of twelve was she, married again only to suffer all this. She will one day hang herself just like our Bachli..."

In one day, Gomti's so-called ill deeds were carried far and wide. Her old mother became nervous with despair. "Come Gomti, let me escort you to your home. Live or die, as is in your sad fate; but go1 there, you must..."

Knotting up a handful of hard walnuts and a pomegranate for Kunnu, Gomti left the next day, accompanied by her mother. All along the way she remained lost in thoughts...

If only she had a proper home, she would call her short-sighted mother to live with her. At least they would all be together even if they were fated to die. Mother too would be contented. But, alas! In her husband's house Gomti's own survival was questionable. As long as her mother remained alive there was at least another door to knock at, another refuge to sun to. The day she died, even that would be gone.

Seeing Gomti's eyes filled with sorrow, her mother wept silently. Consoling her as best as she could, she tried to buoy her fallen spirits.

"Show Pirma to the witch doctor and get him to drive away the evil spirit possessing him. If he could be cured, your misfortune would end. I will take your uncle-in-law to task for ill-treating the offsprings of others, beating them so mercilessly, 'May he be struck with leprosy'. Just because we are poor, he has no business to think that our flesh and blood are made of stone and clay?"

THREE

The evening sun was setting behind the mountains. A thin veil of mist had descended. The snow-capped peaks beyond were struck turmeric yellow by the descending fire ball. Cold and dense darkness had enveloped the cedar forest. Crossing the river Josyuda, Gomti reached her village Ladhaun to find it in the grip of panic.

Different tales on different tongues.

Kaliya-Ka[12] had opened fire with a volley of abuses.

"What good is the birth of such an offspring?"

"I always said that this good-for-nothing fool, this addict, will bring a bad name to the family one day. Now the whole village has earned a bad name, because of him..."

Kaliya-Ka's wife, her skin blacker than coal, flailed the air with her fat arms.

"This 'patwari' is another one. He had first nabbed our Tejuva and was taking him to the lock-up. Had the 'sarpanch' not intervened, our Tejuva would be behind bars..."

Gomti barely reached her own front yard when little Kunnu shot out from the crowd and came towards her. Wrapping himself around her feet like a frightened puppy, he sobbed.

---

12. 'Ka' - Short for Kaka (uncle)

"Ija, they all got together and beat my 'Bajyu'[13]. They put his hands in iron clasps and took him away..."

Gomti's mouth fell open, "Why did they take away your father? Why?"

Torn with anxiety she cornered Harali and begged her to speak out...

Just then Harali's father Khimu-Ka stormed up to them. Waving his small black finger in the air he fumed.

"Hell and damnation upon this Kaliya! Somebody steals and another suffers the punishment? This son-of-a-sow has sent Pirma to the lock-up in place of the real culprit, his own son Tejuva."

A large crowd was spilling into Pirma's front yard, women, men...children...elders...

Suddenly Tejram dashed out of his house, and grabbed Khimu-Ka's neck, slender as a bird's. Twisting it, he dragged the frail old man to one side, "Did you see me stealing, you of low birth? You come on, speak up! Whom have we sent to the lock-up? If Pirma steals, should we suffer the punishment? Out to mislead the whole village, are you?" Khimu-Ka was short-statured, thin as a reed. He was dragged away despite his protests. Hearing the commotion, Kaliya-Ka also reached the spot. His 'hukka' pipe was in his hands, and he cracked it on Khimu-Ka's head...

"You son of an animal, trying to settle old scores? Who will meet out justice? Patwari Jyu or yourself?"

Khimu-Ka was not daunted by the beating from both father and son. Shaking the dust out of his short 'dhoti' he shrieked.

---

13. 'Bajyu' - Father

"I too will see how long you can keep the unfortunate lad in your clutches. I will go to the courts in Lohaghat and Almora to give evidence. I am not my father Harpatiya's true son if I do not tell them the whole truth."

"Be off. I've seen so many of your kind going to the courts. The rascal stole Ganga 'tharu's'[14] cow with its tail chopped...sold it to Laloo 'halwai' in Khatima."

Khimu-Ka raised his folded hands to the heavens. "I swear by the 'Biandhura'[15] that I did not steal the cow. It was your wife who brought shame to you all with that outcaste... The whole 'tharu' settlement had buzzed with tales..."

Maddened with fury at this allegation against his wife, Tejram was about to soar down upon Khimu-Ka like a hawk, when people intervened.

"Khimu-Ka, you are the elder, what are you doing?" Someone pulled him by the arm and took him back to his house, locking him up.

The crowd dispersed. People withdrew behind closed doors. They all feared that the 'patwari' might suddenly descend upon them...The bellows were still. Red hot iron sparks were nowhere to be seen, no sound of hammers on hot iron to be heard. The forges lay stone cold. The entire village of craftsmen-iron-smiths lay silent as though haunted by ghosts. Not a chink of light anywhere.

Gomti's old mother was bone weary. She squatted in the front-yard, clutching her head between trembling hands. Gomti's arms and legs felt as though crushed. She sat helplessly on the earth mound, Kunnu lay sobbing in her lap.

When it was pitch dark, and rain about to pour down, Gomti rose and helped her mother inside.

---

14. 'Tharu' - Tribals living in the 'tarai' area
15. 'Biandhura' - A holy shrine

Spreading a torn 'durrie' on the bedding of rice husk, she put her mother to sleep.

Not a grain of rice in the broken canister...some black 'manduva' flour tied in a knot was as she had left it. The whole day, Pirma had not lighted the fire to cook. She did not have the strength to rise and light the fire to make some fresh 'rotis'. Spreading the grass mat, she too fell upon it to sleep. Kunnu snuggled up to her in the dark, breaking into a sob every now and then.

"Feeling hungry, Kana?" He shook his head.

"Ija!..." he seemed to remember suddenly in the dark, "They beat Bajyu again and again with a stout stick. Then the 'patwari' dragged him a long way, over the mud and stones. Bajyu'sback was bruised and bleeding. Right before everyone he was made to write on a paper, Ija..."

"Sleep. Go to sleep, my lamb," Gomti patted him gently, wiping away her tears.

"Did not your father cook yesterday?"

"No."

"Not today either?"

"No."

"What did you eat then?"

"Harali-Di gave me a cucumber."

"And that is all that you ate in two days...?"

Gomti stroked the child's small face in the dark and drew back her hand in surprise when it felt wet near his eyes.

"Kunnu, are you weeping?"

It was a case of theft of the resin-filled drums lined along the roadside for being transported to Bareilly. Rumour was that the local people had sold twenty, twenty-five drums on the sly to a private truck owner. The incident had taken place near Ladhaun village, and naturally, its residents were suspected.

Pirma had been taken away like this three or four times before too. He would simply submit to all the allegations heaped upon him out of fear of physical torture, and would suffer whatever punishment was meted out to him, returning to his village thereafter. For any theft, any scuffle in the area, a missing horse, cow or goat lifted, Pirma would be nabbed after a cursory investigation and produced before the 'patwari'. The moon-shiners in the woods often took him along with them. They would give him 'ganja' to smoke, food to eat, so that if ever there was a police raid, Pirma would be produced to shoulder the blame. Why this injustice was done to him, nobody cared about nor protested. This time Khimu-Ka's outburst had stunned everyone. All knew that if this frail and short man ever opposed anyone, he was bound to stir up trouble.

Early next morning Kaliya-Ka herded together a few village elders and came to Khimu-Ka's doorstep. Remaining in the background, Kaliya-Ka coaxed the others forward.

"Khimram, we are sorry for Kalram's misdeed yesterday, yaar."

Premram pleaded in deep, sombre tones.

"We beg your pardon on his behalf. If you go to give evidence in the courts in Lohaghat-Champavat, the 'patwari' and the police will come down upon the village again and harass the folk. When Pirma has confessed to being the culprit, why should you poke your nose in the affair? What difference does it make whether Pirma goes to jail or Tejuva? They are brothers, after all. So what if they are sons of two brothers? Pirma is good for nothing, how does it matter if he wiles away some time in jail? Tejuva is a hard-working fellow, he has to go down to the foothills on the thirteenth of this month to muster up his livestock. Why snatch away his livelihood? What wrong has he done to you?"

Short statured Khimu-Ka retorted sharply, "You also know that Tejuva is involved in the theft!"

"You are the limit, he is still a child! He must have fallen into bad company..."

This time when Kalram spoke, Harram scolded him.

"You be quiet, Kalram..."

Khimu-Ka turned to make a face at Kaliya-Ka.

"Still a ch-h-i-l-d, is he? Are you not ashamed, Kalram, marking thy forehead with sandalwood paste, wearing the holy thread of six strings round your neck, and knocking at the doors of lonely women in the night?"

Khimu-Ka was bursting with rage, his beady eyes shooting angry sparks. In a challenging stance, waving his finger in the air as usual, he spilt his fury.

"You hit Pirma on the head with a heavy stone; that is why he has not been the same ever since! Murderer! You are a murderer! You are guilty of murdering a 'brahmin', Kalram! God knows how many you have killed?"

Khimu-Ka's eyes bulged with rage. Stroking his shoulders, Harram pleaded, "Be quiet this time, Khimram. Swear by the mother Ganga, if ever you open your mouth again...," and removing his torn cap from his head, he placed it at Khimu-Ka's feet.

"Have some regard for these white hairs, my friend, Pirma is not being condemned to a life-term, after all. He will be back after a few days of outing. No good prolonging this quarrel needlessly. We will see to Kalram."

Khim-Ka was not in a position to refuse. A sackful of iron utensils lay ready to be taken for sale to Chalsi on the lower side, so that the winter provisions could be purchased and stored. Stroking his white hair, he contained himself with an effort.

FOUR

It rained-all night. It thundered like in hell. Gomti's hut was flooded. The three—mother, daughter and child—squatted at corners, helpless and forlorn. The fury of rain abated by morning. Gomti got busy throwing out the water in panfuls. Kunnu was restless with hunger. Old Ija was unwilling to return to her village.

"How can I leave thee like this, Gomu? What will I do if they drag you away too, just as they have dragged away Pirma?" The old woman said in utter despair.

"No, no Ija, you should go. I will take care if anything happens here. If you stay on, it will cause me needless anxiety. These demons might beat me up and you would not be able to bear it. It will all be painful for you. You must go. Please go."

The earthen floor of the hut was sodden, the firewood damp. The fire-place had been washed away. There was a puddle in its place... How to light a fire? How to give her mother some food? Gomti was at a loss. There was a handful of 'manduva' flour, but the problem was of baking it. How would her toothless mother be able to eat the bathering lumps? Gomti found a stored-away yellow pumpkin. She chopped it up and filled a brass pot with the pieces and took it to Khimu-Ka's house.

She had barely put the vessel on the fire when Kunnu ran up. “Someone has come, Ija. Come home quickly.” Gomti ran home.

“Patwari Jyu has summoned you right away...” one of the visitors informed.

“Why is he calling me?”

“It must be for questioning in connection with the theft case,” the ‘Patwari’s’ assistant, ‘Satwari’ spoke with some authority.

“What questioning?” Ija intervened before Gomti herself could say anything.

“This you had better ask Patwari Jyu himself. It must be something to do with courts. How could we know?”

Gomti worried for a while, then spoke, “Where is he calling me to?”

“To his camp”.

“Is Pirma in lock-up there?” the old woman asked.

“Yes, he has even confessed to the crime.”

“What...?”

“...that he had a hand in the stealing of the resin drums.”

“Then, what is the purpose of calling us?” Gomti lamented helplessly.

“If your words are satisfactory, he might even release your man.”

“What good is such a release? They will drag him away again, whenever they want a scapegoat. I know very well why Patwari Jyu implicates my husband always. Why is he calling me now?”

Just then old Harram came down from his hut. As he walked down, he kept adjusting his torn woollen cap.

"Satwari Jyu is right. Go with him and see, daughter-in-law. There will be justice in the government's 'durbar'..."

"Huh," Gomti was unbelieving and sarcastic, "If there was any justice in the world, would we be suffering like this? There is nothing anything like justice for us...I am going straight to the holy shrine of the God of Gajaar, and, there I will offer rice and wish them ill. Ill, nothing but ill, to those doing injustice. May a curse be wrought upon them, an absolute curse that will cut to their very roots!"

The man who came to summon then left. Ija tried to make Gomti see sense.

"You are needlessly stubborn, Iju. Would they swallow you if you went along? When you went to cook the pumpkin, Sudali was telling me that they have beaten up Pirma so badly that he is vomiting blood. His very life may be in danger..."

"You should leave for home, Ija. Who can change what is our fate? If we are fated to die thus, we shall die thus, that is all..." Gomti, choked with indignation, added, "Why are you worrying yourself to death, Ija?"

Gomti dashed off to Khimu-Ka's house and returned clutching the hot pot of pumpkin with her bare hands. "You must be hungry, Ija. Cool this and eat." Gomti put the pot before her mother. Green pumpkin leaves covered the stew beneath the pot lid.

Her mother could hardly eat. Clutching a hot piece, she tried to cool it by blowing at it. Kunnu, sitting nearby, managed to eat the hot piece. They were beyond noticing the heat of the stew. Gomti laid out the rain-soaked tatters in the sun to dry. She spread the threadbare 'durries' on a pole. She came into the hut.

"You are not eating anything, Ija?"

"My hunger has vanished, Gomu. Should something happen to Pirma, what will you do?" The old woman choked, still holding the uneaten pumpkin piece in her hands.

Mother and daughter sat still for a long time. Gomti broke the silence urging her mother, "It's time for you to return, Ija, otherwise you will not reach home before sunset. You are feeble-sighted and the path along the river is rough and slippery. The rainwater must be flowing waist-high in the streams. Cross them carefully."

Gomti escorted her mother for some distance, then, returned to her hut with a heavy heart, her mind awash with worries. She had not slept the night before, due to the rain havoc. Had Gomti tried to mend her hut? She had often thought of piling a few handfuls of fresh straw upon the roof, and smearing the inside with clay and cow-dung that would keep out the rainwater and the snow, but she had not been able to do it. All the straw that she had gathered, blade by blade, her uncle-in-law had thrown before the oxen while she was away...

Gomti spread out her wet 'ghaghri' to dry in the sun. How to cover her legs now?

She thought for a moment, then unwrapping her long 'pichhaudi'[16] she flung it over her legs. The icy cold caused prickles all over her marble-white, shapely thighs. She tried to stroke some warmth into the skin with her coarse hands. She had nothing to cover herself with, in the coming winter. Her 'ghaghri' was frayed, the 'pichhaudi' was not long enough and her 'angdi'[17] was worn out around the breastcups, only the thin black lining holding together...

16. 'Pichhaudi' - Long head cover

17. 'Angdi' - Bodice-blouse

Gomti had been working in Ramiyan's terraced fields the other day. He went to the lower field and started talking rubbish, his ravenous eyes wandering on her body. Whenever she felt tired of clutching at her torn clothes to cover herself, he eyed her even more intensely. Gomti let her sickle in the fields and went away on the pretence of drinking water. She returned with Ramiyan's wife. They toiled in the fields till night fell.

Whenever Gomti climbed the oak tree to pluck some leaves, the wolf-faced forest guard would lean against the tree and gaze at her... Gomti would spit at him in anger. The rascal laughed shamelessly.

Gomti had dozed in the sun for a while, when Kaliya-Ka came up holding a bundle of green grass. He stood there, letting his eyes devour her from head to foot. Gomti did not know how to cover her body from that wolfish glare.

"Pirma is not yet back from lock-up?"

"N-n-no," Gomti turned her back to him.

She locked her arms around her breasts. She sat still with her eyes closed.

Only when she could sense for certain that Kaliya-Ka had gone, did she rise and dash inside her hut trembling with a strange foreboding that the wicked beast might be up to something devilish.

It might have been a mistake to let Ija go. A mother after all is a mother to protect her child, however weak the mother might appear to be.

FIVE

'Padhani' Jyu, the village head's wife, sent for Gomti to come and work in her field. Gomti went in the hope of earning two 'manduva' rotis by the evening, but her heart was not in her work. She was filled with foreboding. In this whole village, only Khimu-Ka could be expected to side with her, and he had gone down to sell his pots and pans.

An idea flashed in her head. Her hands were still stiff. She stood up.

"I will finish the remaining work tomorrow, 'Padhani' mother-in-law," Gomti pleaded, "...Today I am not feeling too well, my head is dizzy..."

"Are you sure the dizziness is not from an empty stomach?" the 'Padhani' asked.

"No, no, it is not that..." Gomti went on her way home. She had not eaten anything since the day before. Her legs trembled weakly as she plodded up the hill. She saw a cucumber and plucked it. She hid it within the folds of her 'ghaghri'.

Upon reaching her front yard, she found Kunnu lying on her old 'ghaghri' spread out in the sun.

"Are you feverish?" Gomti was out of breath. Kunnu lay still. He stared at her expressionless. Gomti went near and touched his forehead, Kunnu felt hot all over.

She showed him the cucumber she had plucked on the way. He did not bother to reach for it. He looked at the cucumber with disinterest. Gomti went inside searching for something else. Not finding what she searched for, Gomti came out and asked irritably.

"Where is our iron-bowl, Kunuva?" Kunnu rose quickly and brought it out from beneath the broken wooden box. It was filled with apricot stones to play 'Jutti'[18].

"What will you do with it, Ija?"

Gomti did not answer. She pulled together her threadbare dress.

"Will you come, Kuniya?", she asked lovingly.

"Where?"

"Up to the shop in Pokhari."

"What is there, Ija?"

"Nothing, just like that—"

"Will you feed me 'gatta-misri'[19]?" Kunnu asked. Gomti replied ruefully, "If you were fated to eat 'gatta-misri', why would you have been born in this poverty-stricken home?"

It was sunset. It would be dark by the time she returned home. She was uneasy, going all by herself. Who was to be trusted? None, none at all.

"'Thokdar'[20] Jyu! Please write a letter to my brother-in-law Devram. He is posted on the front," and she put out the iron-bowl as an offering, "Please sell this. It will fetch you the price of a letter at least, no?"

---

18. 'Jutti' - A child's game
19. 'Gatta-misri' - Sugar candy
20. 'Thokdar' - Respectable man of the village

Old Kishansingh 'thokdar' knew them to be the unfortunate victims of Kaliya. He had seen Pirma being led away the day before. The 'patwari' and others had assembled at his shop, taking tea, chewing tobacco. Poor Pirma had stood shivering in the cold.

"What is to be written?" he inquired

"Our well-being. That is all."

Taking out the paper, he asked, "You have his address written somewhere?"

Gomti took out a piece of torn paper, faded yellow, from her 'angdi' and spread it out before him.

The 'thokdar' was not very literate. He managed his way somehow. Forty-five years ago he had passed the second class examination from the Khetikhan primary school. That was something, then!

He started writing on a sheet of paper.

Beginning with the ritual 'Swasti Sri', he lifted his heavy head and asked.

"What else do I write?"

That too done, he peered at her again from behind his thick spectacles.

"What more?"

"Write everything," Gomti said.

"There has been no letter from you since the month of 'magha-phalgun'. I got a letter written to you by the 'brahmin' Gahtodi and posted it during the days of the 'Harela' fair. I wonder if you received it at all... Yesterday they took away your 'Thul[21]-Da[22]' again to put him in jail. It

21. 'Thul' - Elder

22. 'Da' - Dada, elder brother

seems to be your uncle's doing. When Khimu-Ka protested, he too was beaten up by the father and son. Your uncle beats us and threatens us. You get your 'sarkar'[23] to write to the 'patwari' here that your elder brother is a simpleton. He did not commit the theft. These people threaten us with 'lathis'. They will finish our existence, one day. Come and look us up, at least once..."

Gomti choked. She could not speak another word. The 'thokdar' went on writing in silence.

In the end, he sealed the letter with a lick, and handed it to her to post.

"Take this O 'Lwari'[24] and drop it in the red drum yonder."

Gomti ran and dropped the letter inside the red letterbox stuck to a pine tree.

The cracked and blackened lamp chimney gave forth a feeble glow. The 'thokdar' was quiet and could not see very far. With a finger sticking out, he asked, "Who is that, woman?"

"The son of your ironsmith, Thokdar Jyu."

After a searching look, the 'thokdar' asked, "What is your name?"

The lad was shy. Hiding half his face in the lapels of his torn coat, he shrugged away.

"Tell him, child. Thokdar Babu wants to know your name," Gomti urged.

Mustering up some courage, the boy whispered "K-u-nu-va".

"What an impressive name you have! Tell me what would you like to eat?"

---

23. 'Sarkar' - Authorities

24. 'Lwari' - Ironsmith's wife

The child looked around with hunger in the eyes. He said haltingly, "Nothing, nothing..."

The old man offered him some peanuts from a bag.

"Come on, eat it. You are shy for no reason. Be my ironsmith, my young friend. Kaliya has fallen to Soban's share." He paused and then spoke again.

"Alright, tell me. Does Kaliya beat you too?"

The little boy nodded "Yes". He squatted like a monkey. He munched the peanuts, shell and all.

"You have fever, and you are eating peanuts? You will get a cough", Gomti warned, but Kunnu did not heed her. He munched on.

◎◎◎

Gomti was startled to find a bundle in the corner of the dark hut.

"What is it?" she wondered.

"It is me—Gomu," was the faint reply.

"Ija? But you had gone!"

The bundle rose, moaning in pain.

"I went as far as Piplati village, and then my feet would not move forward. The village folk there rebuked me—how un-feeling can you be, going home, leaving behind your daughter in hell? What is there for you back home? If you should die, there is none even to drop a few drops of water in your mouth when you breathe your last."

Gomti smuggled up closer.

"Khilanand of Piplati told me that Pirma is in a bad state. He has not been sent to Lohaghat jail, he is still in lock-up in the 'patwari's' camp.

“Khilanand saw it all with his own eyes”, Ija related this massaging her aching feet...

“Who knows, he could be released if you present yourself there once, my child. Why don’t you give your statement? Patwari Jyu too had sent for you. Go and tell them the truth. Tell them, you people did not commit any theft.”

Gomti heard it all in silence. The whole night she was filled with remorse The next day, her heart was not in her work. Her husband’s guileless face haunted her.

In the evening, she sent for Khimu-Ka’s son.

“Devar[25] Jyu[26], will you not take me up to Patwari Jyu’s camp? He had sent for me for questioning.”

“Why not? Come, let us go right now. They say Piram-Da is in a precarious condition”, Karamram said.

“I am going, Ija. I will be back by nightfall. Feed Kunnu and put him to sleep. He has been feverish since yesterday...”

Gomti left in haste, escorted by Karamram.

The old mother boiled a few grains of rice, but Kunnu did not even taste them. Sprinkling a little salt over a bowl of rice water, she sipped it, saving the rice for Gomti. Kunnu, too, would want something to eat in the morning.

Gazing at the stars through a chink in the cracked door-flap she thought—Gomti would have reached there by now. Who knows how late it would be when she returned? The star trinity would be out by then. Securing the latch from inside she had barely dozed when someone knocked at the door flaps. Crawling up in the dark she opened the door and saw—Karamiya stood there.

---

25. ‘Devar’ - Brother-in-law

26. ‘Jyu’ - Ji (suffix for respect)

“Gomu has not come—?”

“Patwari Jyu said that the investigations would take time. She told me—you go, I will come back alone.”

The old woman could ask no more. Closing the door slowly, she rolled over on the ice-cold bed. Tired after the day’s long trek, her feet ached but sleep eluded her. So many questions loomed large before her—pricking her with sharp fangs.

If only the wretch had not been endowed with such beauty, she would not suffer thus—the old mother let out a cold sigh. Memories of her own youth came rushing back...

She was barely seventeen or eighteen. Though married for eight or nine years, she had remained childless. Despite her dark complexion, she glowed with beauty and youthfulness.

Whoever set his eyes upon her could not look away. Such delicate beauty was rare in the community of ironmongers.

Once, upon returning from the ‘Biandhura’ fair, she had found the entire household in distress.

Her sister-in-law had committed suicide by hanging herself from an apricot tree.

Being a widow, she had been treated contemptuously by her in-laws. Her own family would not allow her to stay in their house. To make matters worse, she had become pregnant. To escape the wrath of the community, she had to find a way out, death.

Her death had proved cause enough to harassment of the entire household. The ‘patwari’ and ‘peshkar’ had descended upon them with their retinue. For days they grilled everyone, beating them frequently to extract the truth.

The 'peshkar' had ruled that the girl's family had murdered her. Why would any woman kill herself? Do all unhappy people hang themselves? The dead girl's father, brothers, and all in the family were herded together in a lock-up that was a cattle pen.

The 'peshkar' was fond of liquor. The village folk had been obliged to cater to his weakness. Goats were slaughtered daily and the entire retinue feasted like a marriage party, all expenses borne by the villagers.

When not a single clue could be found, he had taken the 'patwari' to task one night, "Question not only the menfolk but the womenfolk too. Who all are in the house? Drag them out..."

The victim's mother, elder brother's wife had all been called, one by one.

Then it had been her turn.

"She must have had a hand in this murder," the 'Peshkar' had stamped his foot on the ground and thundered.

She had been detained in a dingy hole, till late in the night for questioning.

The grilling session began in the night after meals.

"The girl must have put up a struggle when you must have tied her up by force and hanged her. There must have been a scuffle, between the two of you, definitely. The girl must have been desperate. It is possible that she may have bitten you or clawed you."

"Why should she bite me? I had no quarrel with her", she had begun to answer when the 'peshkar' had gritted his teeth and roared in rage.

"If it was not you, then was it supposed to be me who had a score to settle with her? Daughter-of-a-bitch, your mother-in-law has revealed that the two of you were not on speaking terms!" Thus it went on.

"But that was over a new 'pichhaudi'..."

"What else! Would it be over horses and elephants?"

The 'peshkar' had gesticulated with his hands.

"Thou wouldst deny it now! Of doubtful birth, you, now trying to act as innocent as a cow, art thou? The village folk have told me all about you."

"There are shocking stories about you... There is not a man whom you have not lured..."

The 'peshkar' had panted after the outburst. He made a curious sight, sipping cold water even in that cold weather. After a brief pause, he had thundered on, again.

"Come on show me, where are the scratches on thy body after the scuffle? There should be teeth-marks, nail scratches somewhere. My hair has not turned white in the sun. I have made many fearsome dacoits turn around. You are just a bird, a mere bird I could rub you between my fingers and you would not be traceable."

She had stared at him, stupefied– what was he saying?

It was all beyond her grasp. Fearfully, haltingly, she had pleaded, "Why would I kill my sister-in-law? Why would I engage in a scuffle with her? I am not to blame, have mercy, Sire!"

Beseeching him with folded hands, she had wept, hoping that he might relent and let her off. A stinging slap had landed on her cheek and the 'peshkar' had threatened.

"Acting innocent after doing away with your sister-in-law? You daughter-of-a-sow take your clothes off. Show me the scuffle marks. My name is not Kunwar Singh 'Peshkar' if I do not have you hanged the same way."

She had trembled with fright. Not only the slapped cheek but her whole body ached. Stars exploded before her eyes.

"Off with your clothes!"

Mechanically, she pulled 'pichhaudi' covering her head on one side.

"Will your father come here to pull off the 'angdi'?" Without any protest, she had put away that too. Then, whatever he had ordered to be removed, she did helplessly. The undressing over, he lifted the hurricane lantern and scrutinised her body, looking for a tell-tale mark. He pretended to inspect her body all over again for evidence of her so-called crime.

"The village-folk are right. You are a sly one, a cunning witch. Killed your sister-in-law and not a scratch on your body? Come on, tell me, how did you put the noose around her neck? Come on tell me, tell me."

When her eyes had brimmed over again with tears, the 'peshkar' pretended to comfort her by lifting up her naked body and laying it on his bed...

"Must be tired... Rest now. I will ask the rest of the questions in the morning..." He then put out the lantern for the night.

Then, as long as the 'peshkar' was camped there, he continued to interrogate her with all his wicked variations. In the end, on his day of departure, he had told her condescendingly, "I have saved your family from being sentenced to death, only because of you, otherwise you would have become a widow at this tender age."

Then for her body, the torture for herself did not end there. The 'patwari' took over...

The morning star was clearly visible in the sky.

Gomti had not returned yet. The old mother transfixed her dull gaze beyond the door, lost in thought.

Gomti at last returned home, leading her sick, dazed husband by the hand. The old woman saw sadness incarnating as her daughter Gomti was pale, her face mirrored a strange bitterness.

While Gomti changed her clothes, her old mother spotted tiny droplets of blood around the numerous nail scratches all over her body.

SIX

Pirma's health improved within a few days. Gomti's bruises also healed.

One day she had barely returned home, weary after a day's back-breaking labour in another's fields, when Khimu-Ka's daughter Harali ran to her and burst out, "What are you doing sitting here, Bojyu[27]? All of them are beating up Pirma-Da near our walnut field; I was bringing the goats home when I heard Tejuva-Da saying, 'Let us kill and bury the rascal in the pit here'..."

Hearing this, Gomti shot like an arrow through the fields, Kunnu following. Darkness was descending. It had rained a while ago and the winding narrow mud pathway was slushy. Crossing puddles, stones, all Gomti raced to the spot and reeled in horror upon seeing a blood-curdling sight. Pirma lay on the wet ground writhing in pain like an earthworm trampled under foot. Kaliya-Ka was beating him relentlessly.

"You low-bred rascal, did I let you take the animals to pasture for this? The potato fields are ruined! I will bleed you to death today..."

"What are you doing?" Gomti panted up and shrieked in panic.

---

27 'Bojyu' - Sister-in-law (brotber's wife)

"Are you out to kill him?"

Kaliya-Ka spat out a filthy abuse, then mouthing slander against Gomti's mother, the most shameful relationship between her and his bull, he hissed, "Thinking yourself to be the daughter of a barrister are you? Today I will do away with you too. Wanton hussy, once widowed, now going wild with youth? God knows where she roams the whole day long!"

As Gomti bent to help Pirma rise from the wet ground, Tejuva twisted her arm and flung her far in the field, "Our entire crop ruined because of this rascal! Was this useless animal sent to the field to snuggle up in the blanket and sleep? The village herds have ruined all the fields, not a single plant left..."

"Mercy on me, forgive him this time" Gomti begged wiping the mud from Pirma's body.

"He is gripped with fever for the last few days...he spends the whole night shivering...he might not have been able to recover from the convulsions. I will pay back every single pie of the loss you have suffered, even if I have to work in other's fields, I swear by the god of 'Biandhura'..."

"This naked hussy will make good our loss..." Tejram jeered at her.

"Get away you slut, or should I trample you too in this?" He kicked Pirma who groaned as the pain tore through him.

"O-o. I-j-a-a-!"

"O, you people of this village, do you hear? These people are killing us..." Gomti cried when suddenly a torch beam flashed on the path in front.

"What is happening? What goes on here?" A man ran towards the site. No one recognised his voice, but when he drew near, they saw him in the light of the torch. He was Devram, Pirma's younger brother.

Dressed in army uniform he gazed at them in surprise... Each one stood rooted to the spot, wooden with amazement.

Pirma lay half-buried in the mud, his face hidden between his knees. Kaliya-Ka's lathi hung in the air, his hands clutching it. Tejram stood still, a wet shoe raised in one hand...

"Why, what has happened, Bojyu?" Devram turned towards Gomti.

She broke into hysterical sobbing, "Devar Jyu, we have been suffering this torture ever since you went away to the front..."

Devram was shocked to hear his sister-in-law's heart rendering wail. Coldly summing up the entire situation, he demanded, "What is wrong Kaka? Why are you beating him...?"

"..."

Raising his eye brows he rebuked, "Call yourself a religious man? Even your moustache has turned white, yet you have no shame, whatsoever! beating up this poor mindless being so mercilessly?"

"Why? I ask you, Why?"

"What would you know? He let all our fields be ruined today,"

Tejram rushed forward to side with his father, but Devram pulled him by the collar of his torn coat, and gave him such a resounding slap with his trained, powerful hands that Tejuva went rolling into the 'manduva' field nearby.

"Kaka, you are of my father's age, I have looked upon you as my father, otherwise I would have slashed you into a thousand pieces and flung them all over the field..."

Controlling his rage, Devram turned to Gomti, "Come Bojyu, let us go home."

Lifting his brother from the ground Devram saw that he still trembled from a terrible fright. His hands, feet and face were besmeared with blood...

He could not even be recognised. Pulling out a clean khaki duster from his bag, Devram began wiping his brother's face. Leading him by the hand he reached the crossroads, when all of a sudden there was a rustling noise beneath the pear tree, as though a hare had scampered away. Devram flashed his torch...

Gomti told him, "Must be our Kunuva."

Kunnu came out of hiding. He had taken shelter behind a tree, like a frightened lamb.

Devram asked, "Why were you hiding?" Kunnu was too terror-stricken to reply. Gomti explained, "He must have been terrorised by the beating. Once before he remained hidden in a pile of straw outside, the whole night."

Devram reached out and caught him, lifting the child in his arms. The starched uniform got smudged, but he could not have cared less.

◎◎◎

A small hut thinly patched up, the stored grain barely enough to fill the bowl of a dried-up gourd, a few broken utensils, some tatters slung on the rope stretched across—the abode was exactly as he had left it before going to the front.

Devram's bride had died and he had not remarried.

Gomti would bring up the topic in every letter, but gradually it was ignored. Kalkot, Bhingrada, Rotyuda, Bhaunra—proposals came from so many places, but he had turned them down. Whenever Gomti brought up the topic, he would reply, "What is the use, Bojyu? My mind has changed altogether. Life on the front is so uncertain.

I will roam the front and none to look after the woman I marry at home. See what happened in Sunder-Ka's home. Kaki[28] began living with another man within a year only."

"So what? Do army people never marry?"

"Why not? But each to his own belief. If I do get a nice girl I will not say no, but I know there will never be anyone like the one I want..." and Devram would laugh mischievously.

This time there was a proposal from Gomti's own village. The girl was from a respectable family, wise and of clean habits, well trained in household chores. Gomti had planned that if Devram returned safely this time, she would put shackles on his feet!

She broached the subject at mealtime, but Devram was unwilling.

"I have changed my mind, seeing all this, Bojyu. You people are no better off, why add another member?"

He continued to eat in silence the hot, puffed 'rotis' of wheat flour.

He knew that there was nothing in the house. The flour had been borrowed from Khimu-Ka's place. It would be paid for out of the earnings from the next day's labour in someone else's field.

"I got Thokdar Jyu to write a letter to you. Did you get it, Lala[29]?"

"No, Bojyu", Devram replied, "There was no news of you people for such a long time that I was worried. Wondered whether Thul-Da was unwell."

---

28. 'Kaki' - Aunt
29. 'Lala' - Usually a form of addressing a trader but used here as an endearment for brother-in-law.

After a moment's thought, he asked quietly, "How is Thul-Da, anyway?"

"See for yourself." Gomti sighed deeply. "He remains sitting wherever he is made to, mute as an animal without hands or feet, not caring for food or drink. A puff of 'ganja-attar[30]', and not a care in the world. Your Kaka is taking full advantage of it all, makes your brother mind the potato fields all night and take the animals to pasture during the daytime. When I protest, he lunges at me with an axe to chop off my head. You saw it all today——their cruelty; stone-hearted brutes, they be... How can they bring themselves to raise their hands against your brother?"

"They're terrorising us all the time!"

Gomti pushed up her blouse and showed her back "See, what murderers they are!"

Devram was stunned, rendered speechless for a long time. Seeing Bojyu's back streaked blue, his eyes seemed to bleed.

"What should I do, Bojyu? I could have lynched them, pumped bullets into them, but my own discipline pulled me back. Oh, conscience, too! I cannot raise my hands against Kaka. He is our father's age, this thought holds me back. They are feelingless brutes, worse than animals, but should we too be like them?"

Gomti stared vacantly at her brother-in-law's face.

After washing his hands, Devram began searching for the key to his trunk.

"Bojyu, did you never get Thul-Da treated?"

"Of course. I did everything, Devar Jyu. I tried medicines, I got the evil spirits driven out of him. The animal doctor's treatment continued for a while ..."

---

30. 'Ganja-attar' - Hashish and dried juice of 'Bhang'.

"You are another one, Bojyu! The animal doctor is for beasts, not humans!" Devram interrupted her.

"We are not humans, Devar Jyu," replied a depressed Gomti, "I swear by the shrine of Binandhura, your brother's condition did improve with the animal doctor's treatment. Your Kaka could not bear it, so he spread false tales about him and me. The poor man is a 'brahmin' by caste. When they started besmirching his name, he stopped coming over here altogether."

Devram was upset at not finding the key. Gomti suggested that they look for it by daylight. The cooking fire was dying out and nothing was visible in the dark.

"Let me give some sweetmeats to the child at least."

At last, he found the key in the hip pocket of his pants, and he quickly unlocked his trunk.

The 'pedas' bought in Tanakpur market were in a plastic bag. These he spilt out on a piece of paper. Kunnu began stuffing his mouth full with both hands. Gomti tasted just a little. Devram placed a few pieces on Thul-Da's palm.

Seeing them remain thus for quite some time, Devram nudged him gently, "Thul-Da, what are you staring at? Why don't you eat?"

Devram's Thul-Da was lost in a world of his own.

T-u-p-p, T-u-p-p, two drops slid from his eyes and fell on the sweetmeats.

SEVEN

The fellows had been working since early morning, the iron-smiths had their forges belching fire. The red-hot iron let off sparks at each blow of the heavy hammer.

Devram remained in his courtyard, not wishing to go out to meet anyone. Spreading out his army blanket in the sun, he sprawled on it. He had never imagined that things could have so worsened back home...

—The hut needs repair. How will these people manage when it snows in the winter?

—Thul-Da has to be taken to the Mayawati Hospital. That is where he would get some free treatment. His brain might start functioning properly once the body is strong.

—The 'thokdar' of Pokhari is to be paid back a portion of the old loan. At least some of the interest should be paid, otherwise he will harass these people when I am gone, Devram thought.

—The three well-watered fields, in Gajaar, ideal for paddy cultivation, are mortgaged with Kaka. If they could be freed, the problem of their survival at least would be solved. How long could they go on working in other people's fields?

—The 'patwari' will have to be pulled up. If he messes up again, I will get a letter of complaint written from my regiment to the deputy collector, Devram decided.

—Kaka will have to be warned not to raise his hands to them again. Now that the house and land have been divided, why should he make them work for him without remuneration? After all, what did Kaka give them at the time of dividing the property? Not even some proper utensils. He grabbed them all.

The same evening Devram brought a milch goat from the Kamlek lowland. Kunuva could take it to graze over the arid wasteland, and Thul-Da would taste one or two sips of the milk now and then.

A 'kurta' and pajama for Thul-Da, 'dhoti' and blouse for Bojyu. For Kunnu he had already purchased a pajama length in Bareilly.

"If I am transferred to Ambala Cantonment, Bojyu, I will call Thul-Da there and have him treated. Do not despair. Thul-Da will work in the fields as he did long ago. I will send you eight, or ten maunds of iron from the wholesalers. If he can beat out a few pots and pans, it should bring enough money for food and clothing."

Devram was home for barely six days and making plans when the postman came from Khetikhan to deliver an important letter "REPORT TO THE REGIMENT IMMEDIATELY..."

Devram sat stunned.

The danger of foreign invasion increased each day. Newspapers and the radio spilt forth ominous news. An explosion could occur at any time—but he had never imagined that the situation would become critical so soon. This time he was to be home on a full two months' leave. He had planned to meet all relatives, and if anything was settled, he would not turn down a match either, but now all he could think of was his regiment.

He went around meeting people during the short time he had left with him, requesting the village elders never to let Kaliya raise his hands against his brother and his family. He told all who got together in the market place of Pokhari and Dhoonighat about Kaliya-Ka's black deeds; the 'Sarpanch' and the chairman of the village council too were apprised of the situation.

The sun had not risen. A dense fog hung all around. Pirma carried a small trunk and bedding wrapped in a durrie. Gomti walked alongside, leading her small son. Devram walked briskly ahead, taking steady and fast strides, all spit and polish, in his army uniform. His heavy boots crunched on the narrow stony pathway. A bus would be leaving Pokhari for Tanakpur soon, and he was in a hurry.

Putting his luggage atop the bus, Devram scrambled down. Taking out some currency notes from his pocket he handed them to Pirma who stood between despair and hope. "Why do you lose heart, Thul-Da? If they raise their hands, why do you not wield your axe and do a war dance? Slice off their heads...I will save you from the gallows. Yes, I will! A man dies but once Thul-Da..."

"If only he could do this, Lala, we would not be treated thus. You go in peace, do not worry about us. We will overcome whatever is in store for us. Do not leave with a heavy heart..."

The bus moved. Devram jumped onto it and took his seat. As the bus moved downwards, he wondered whether the front at home was not many times more formidable than the front at Chushul. Battle at home, front at the border!

His village, his fields, his trees and mountains, all gradually receded from his view. He looked at the receding landscape with mounting nostalgia. He knew not why he was nagged by a strange notion. Could this be the last time he was to see his birthplace?

EIGHT

Kaliya-Ka fumed. Everyone in the Pokhari market place had derided him.

"They say that Devram has got an official letter written, O, Kalram. Not only Patwari Jyu, but even you are going to be in hot water. You will be handcuffed and Tejuva will go to jail and grind grain and crush bamboo for making rope. You beat up not only Pirma but his wife too? If ten witnesses get together in the village, there will not even be a pond for you to drown yourself. Your high-handedness will come to an end, you will know the full reckoning", Kishansing 'thokdar' drew on his 'hukka'.

"Come on, Thokdar Jyu, how can you talk like this? Pirma and Tejuva are equal in my eyes. Who does not keep his children in line, tell me? If I have advised them sometimes for their own good what tyranny have I wrought on them?" Kalram tried to settle the argument.

"But what harm has that woman done to you? She was wailing here the other day, poor thing," the 'thokdar' coughed.

"You should not torture anyone Kalram. You are our iron-smith, that is why we advise you."

"Now what can I say, Thokdar Sahib," Kalram shrugged, "Hers is a different story altogether...a woman of ill-repute. How can I reveal my household scandals in public? She has a thousand affairs blooming. I will tell you everything in private one day, then you too will concede that your Kalram is right."

"She had a different story to tell about you. Never mind, how does it concern us anyway?" The 'thokdar' clutched his black coconut 'chillum' and threw up whiffs of grey smoke. Drying his wet hands over the fire in the tea stall nearby, Gumansingh intervened. "We believe all that you say, Kalram, but, yaar, swear by the goddess 'Bhagwati', and explain why you make that hapless fool work free for you. That poor fellow has a family. They are reduced to begging for foodgrains... Kaliya-Ka lost patience.

"You say this without knowing all the facts, 'padhan' (head-man). Do you know who bore the cremation expenses of Pirma's mother?" Patting his chest, Kaliya-Ka boasted, "I took a loan to put a shroud on that sinner. Nobody talks of repaying that. If I take a little work out of them now and then, by way of interest, it pricks everyone." Kalram prepared to rise.

Settling the flaps of his coarse woollen wrap on his shoulders, he said, "'Padhan', you are our esteemed elder. Don't get upset about it. The people of Ladhaun and Kamlek are envious that Kalram should be comfortably off, that is all."

Kalram did not stay long. Devram had taken the matter up at the government level; this fact was like a broken thorn embedded in his flesh.

Debiya is not bad. Pirma is a simpleton. Only this hussy is the root of all bad blood. She alone has incited Debiya and has brought me a bad name. Cursed be me if I do not strip her naked in front of ten people and give her a sound thrashing with a thornbush stick, Kalram vowed to himself. As long as she stays, there will be no peace for me. She must be got rid of. Either she dies, or leaves the village—it has to be one way or the other...

Kalram sat alone in the dark, gnashing his teeth, when Tejuva came to inform him that Debiya had lodged a complaint against them with the 'patwari' as well.

◎◎◎

That night when it rained, Tejuva crept out stealthily in the dark with his father, both holding spades, and begin digging a drain in the 'kucha' front yard in such a way that the surrounding water would flood Pirma's hut. The water flow changed course and entered the hut. Soon the household goods were afloat—beddings, utensils, all floated around. The supporting poles of the hut would have come crashing down when Gomti jumped out, axe in hand, braving the heavy downpour. Removing the pile of earth frantically with both her hands, she changed the course of the drain. Panting, she came in drenched from head to toe. The hut was full of mud and everything was wet.

Nothing remained, no flour, no rice, no salt, no oil... Wrapped in thin tatters, she shivered with the cold, Kunnu had leapt atop the wooden box, like a monkey, and had pulled the little kid into his lap. Picking up a pan, Pirma helped Gomti to throw out the water. The goat bleated away in knee-deep water.

Three or four days later, Gomti returned from the water-mill one night after grinding some coarse grain and found Kunnu sobbing in the front yard.

"What happened, Kuna?"

"Our goat died, Ija," Kunnu wiped his running nose with his torn sleeve.

Kunnu sat stroking the dead goat's ice-cold back, spilling out his heartache. The kid lay dead. "I had tied them to the plum tree and had gone to fetch water from the brood. I cut a bundle of fresh grass too...and carrying water and grass I returned and found these two sprawled like this. When Teju-Ka heard, he told someone that the snake must have bitten them... Only the day before he had seen a black viper beneath the plum tree."

Gomti's eyes welled up with tears of blood clutching her head, she squatted beside Kunnu.

"When you were returning with the grass, did you see any one near the plum tree?"

'Teju-Ka was going up with quick steps, his plough on his shoulders..."

"From which side?"

"By the path running along the plum tree..."

Soon a large crowd had gathered. It was anybody's guess whether the goats were bitten by a snake. Their colour was blue, their mouths frothy...

Gomti knew the truth, but who would side with her?

Her lips were sealed, she sat numbed with shock.

Sometimes a bowl would vanish, another time a ladle. The torn scrap of durrie was put out in the sun to dry, by evening that too had gone. She had made a big pile of dry wood for a warm winter. This too was reduced to a quarter of its size within a few days. Gomti bore the ravages in silence. Saying a few words. Gomti would stir up a hornet's nest. At first, only one or two from that house came and bullied them but now the whole lot of them, big and small, would swoop down upon them like kites and crows. The village folk were too scared to utter a word. Whenever there was trouble, they would hide behind closed doors, fearing that should someone be wounded or murdered they would be called to court to give evidence.

Gomti suffered the agony of it all somehow, but one day the ground gave way beneath her. It was like a bolt from the blue—an official letter from the front in Pirma's name—Sipahi Devram has achieved martyrdom on the front against Pakistan.

Gomti saw stars in daytime, plunged into a bottomless pit of despair. She knew only too well that her brother-in-law's threats had been their feeble protection so far, and now even that was gone. Gomti's eyes were drained of tears. She could not weep, no matter how much she wanted to. She went about agonizingly performing all the rites—

A lamp was lighted over a small mound of barley in one corner. Pirma's head was shaved, and wrapping a coarse woollen shawl about him, he sat in mourning. Relatives and friends came to grieve with Pirma, but none from Kaliya's family turned up.

There was nothing in the house and, therefore, the two remaining fields had been mortgaged with the 'thokdar'. Gomti did not allow a single lapse. The complete cremation rites were performed. She arranged for all that was needed, not forgetting to buy a calf for fifteen rupees. It was to be set free on the thirteenth day, symbolic of the dead man's soul being released of worldly ties.

Devram had been home on leave barely a couple of months ago...Gomti could not bring herself to accept the fact that he was now gone for ever. Her frenzied mind was torn with doubts—could it be a mischief monger's trick? A false alarm? Enemies surrounded them on all sides, whom to trust, whom not to trust?

It was heard that Kaliya-Ka had guffawed with glee, "The hussy had become vain. Let us see which of her husbands comes to her rescue now..."

All returned home after the cremation rites. An overpowering loneliness filled the house. They had not eaten a morsel, and went to sleep on empty stomachs.

Their sole source of strength had gone. That young man on whom was faith pinned was gone. With her face in her palms, Gomti sobbed. Pirma stared away in the dark. Kunnu slept on a dirty piece of sacking nearby, tired after the day. He had gone along with everyone for the last rites. Back home he had asked Gomti, "Will Kaka never return, Ija?"

The whole village slept. The whole world seemed to have gone to sleep. The night seemed darker than usual, perhaps it was a moonless night.

Footsteps sounded on the dry grass outside. Before Gomti could stretch out to peep, there was a loud voice and the flimsy door flap lay broken.

"Where is the bitch? Come out..." Tejuva thundered. He had a lighted torch of the pine bark and a large sickle in one hand. Pulling the sleeping woman by her hair with the other hand, he snarled, "For whom do you weep here, you of lowly birth? Come to my house, from today you will be my mistress. You can warm my bed. I cannot wait till Pirmuva dies..."

Gomti cried in fear. Kunnu screamed. She struggled to free her hands, but his vicious grip tightened.

As she was dragged away, she looked pleadingly at Pirma, begging for help, but he sat motionless on his bed—his head buried between his knees. The heart-rending cries in the dark awakened so many neighbours from their sleep. They rushed towards Pirma's hut, hurriedly flinging their wraps around them.

Tejuva was hell-bent to kill or die. Swinging the sickle he threatened, "Beware! I will chop down whosoever steps forward...This is our family affair...a private matter. None is to interfere."

Dragging out Gomti by her arm, he entered his house and bolted die door with a loud bang.

Everything happened in a blink, the village folk stood around, non-plussed.

Gomti struggled with all her might. Defeated and rendered senseless, she rolled over. Tejuva tore her clothing into shreds, and gagging her, came down on her with sheer brute force, a display of animal lust. Gomti's naked body glowed in the yellow light of the pine bark torch. He stared at her with the greed of a ferocious maneater. Gomti stirred, moaning in pain. Her eyelids flickered and Tejuva's face loomed before her. Suddenly her whole body seemed on fire. A current raced through her and her eyes blazed with hatred. She leapt upon Tejuva like a hungry lioness and slapped the flaming torch onto his face. She dug both her palms so fiercely into his neck that his body gradually turned limp, and with a groan caught in his throat, he rolled over to one side.

Gomti's fingers searched desperately for the bolt in the dense darkness. Grabbing a thin sheet that lay nearby, she flung it hastily upon her body, and leapt out like a wild cat.

Kaliya-Ka went after her with a chopper, but she bolted away, and vanished into the dense wild forest.

NINE

—Gomti drowned in the river.

—Gomti jumped over a precipice. The shepherds had seen a pack of vultures hovering around the steep slopes of the pine forests.

—A maneater in the jungle devoured Gomti.

Many tongues, many stories.

Tejram did not emerge from his hut for many days. The pine bark torch had singed his face horribly. His neck bore deep nail marks. He had barely escaped death that day; had she clutched at his throat a little longer, God knows what would have happened.

Tejuva had imagined that he could terrorize Gomti into living with him. She would whimper and whine for a few days. Then submit, that is what he had thought. She was but a woman, all would be forgotten once the belly was full, what attachment could she have, after all, for that imbecile Pirma, who could not even look after himself? What would Gomti do with such a spouse?

The other day she had been bathing on the broad river bank.

Crushing the gummy roots of the 'vadeal' tree by beating them on a stone she had been washing her hair with them, looking entirely beautiful in her flimsy wraps. The youthful figure, the body carved as though from marble—he had been blinded, absolutely blinded...

His infatuation had caused him such deep embarrassment, that he had been wounded not only in body but deep within... His muscles would ripple with the desire for revenge, but she was beyond reach...

Barely a fortnight later someone brought news to the village that Gomti had not died, but had started living with the ironsmith Khushal of Narsing Danda; the fellow had seen it all with his own eyes...

Kaliya-Ka's tongue lashed out, "Arre Bhauna (the Goddess Bhavani), these are what they call a woman's wiles. Son, I knew it all along. This flirt had a lover. She just wanted an excuse to break free."

Kaliya-Ka had been a man of shrewd manipulation all his life. He knew well when and how to play his trumps. How would he tolerate it that Gomti should start living with Khushal, just like that?

He flared up at the news. Tejram too saw clearly the opportunity to take his revenge.

For a couple of days, they planned their strategy to twist her around; they took along five or six local youths and set out for Narsing Danda.

Kaliya-Ka roared his challenge from the front yard, "O, Khushiya, who are you to keep a daughter-in-law of my family in your house? Come out, I will settle the score with you..."

There was a function in Khushalram's house and he had guests—all friends and relatives. Standing behind the wooden railing he answered.

"You toothless old man, have you come for your daughter-in-law today? You, exploiter of your own nephew, now want to ravish her. I'd be a dog if I do not break your leg and send you limping back...your corpse will go out of Narsing Danda today..."

The verbal warfare was continuing when Gomti was seen coming out of the animal's enclosure, a pile of grass on her head. Tejram pounced upon her like a hawk. Flinging aside the bundle of grass he cursed, "Pariah bitch, get home. Has Piramuwa taken thee in marriage or this rascal Khushal? Your fate will be decided by the 'panchayat' there."

Seeing Tejram pulling Gomti, the youths who had accompanied him also started pulling Gomti towards the path leading home.

"Let go, you black monster, let go of me! Call yourself a brother, my brother-in-law? You are a blot on the family name!"

Showering abuses, Gomti sunk her teeth into Tejram's wrist.

"Worms will crawl your body, worms! You ugly devil, let go of me..."

Khushal lost his wits for a moment. He jumped down the wooden railings of the balcony. In the paved courtyard below lay three or four stout poles for flailing the grain. Picking up one, Khushal came leaping like a deer across the terraced fields...

He landed a heavy blow on Kalram's bent back, and lunged towards Tejram when someone held his hand from behind, "What are you doing, O, Khushal-Da? What if someone dies...?"

The son of Khushal's maternal uncle was about to say something else, but Khushal pushed him aside.

More people from the village rushed over toting poles and sticks—it was a question of prestige of the entire village.

Tejram bore the shower of lathi blows, but did not let Gomti's wrist slip from his grasp. In the scuffle, Khushal's younger brother landed such a staggering blow on Tejram's chest that he doubled up into a heap.

To avenge this, Kaliya-Ka picked up a large boulder with both hands and hit Khushal's brother with it. Soon there were about five persons injured and bleeding. By then the village head and elders intervened and the heat ebbed a little.

"When my nephew was wed to this woman, how can she live here in Khushal's house?" A panting Kaliya-Ka addressed the 'padhan' of the village as he shook the dust out of his clothes.

"Kaliya rascal, do you treat her as your daughter-in-law?"

Khushal thundered, "You are worse than an animal. I declare openly that she shall not return to your village. Do what you can..."

"How will she not return with us...?" Tejram had recovered somewhat by then and twitching his shoulders, he said, "It is no joke to keep someone else's wife in one's home?"

"Go then you one-eyed rascal, do what you can. The doors of Lohaghat and Champawat courts are open. I care a hoot for the likes of you..."

Khushal wriggled his thumb at Tejram eyeing them all with pure hatred.

"Yaar, Khushal..." an old gentleman from Narsing Danda intervened, "Be fair. Don't get worked up, yaar, truth is truth."

“Alright, you say, how can you keep someone’s wedded wife in your house? If you have to keep her, then you will have to pay compensation. You will have to deposit ‘dhadi’ (the price of keeping such a woman) in the presence of the ‘panchayat’ members.”

“If you people say so, I will do that, but from now on if these people touch her, I shall behead each one of them. Do not hold me responsible then...”

“Come hither, behead me! Let me see!” Tejram glared arrogantly and challenged. A supporter from the opposite camp slapped his thighs and came forward to knock him down.

“Quiet, be quiet.” His companion led him far away.

Both sides conferred again for a compromise. Eventually, it was decided that the ‘dhadi’ was mutually acceptable. The ‘panchayat’ sat in judgement in Keshavram’s covered verandah. Gomti, too, was called to put her thumb on the paper.

It was decided that Khushalram would pay four hundred rupees to Kalram, who on behalf of Pirma would affix his signatures on the ‘panchayatnama’ (the written permission of the Village Committee of five members). Thereafter Pirma would have no right over Gomti. She would live in Khushalram’s house—as his wife. He would be responsible for supporting her...

Khushalram put the ‘dhadi’ receipt in his inner pocket and flung the cash amount on Kalram’s face.

“The money is not yours, Kalram...”

Baring his yellowed, dirty teeth in a sly grin, Kalram replied, “All within the family...Pirma could not come, being unwell. We will hand over the money to him when we reach back ... How does it matter? It is all within the family.”

Kaliya-Ka laughed all the way home!

◎◎◎

He had proved his devilish cunning, turning loss into victory, extorting so much while coming away...

Out of the money, Pirma was given a vest to wear, and a cheap, flimsy 'kurta' dangled from Kunnu's neck.

—Kunuwa would now take the herds out grazing.

—Pirma was to help in the smithy. He could work the bellows all day.

TEN

Gomti had nothing to wear. She had been covering herself somehow in hand-me-downs. Khushal brought her some garments from the Khetikhan market. He bought two thin silver bangles from Nandlal, the goldsmith, picking up eight, ten glass bangles also on his way back. Never before, in all her life, had Gomti worn such beautiful garments, the colour of butterfly wings, all shiny! When she wore them, her beauty took on a new dazzle. The white stone in her nose stud looked like a drop of milk. She would feel it, over and over again...

Seeing her reflection in the mirror, Gomti stood transfixed. She was filled with a wondrous delight, which slowly gave way to a strange melancholy. Her face drained of colour. This beauty was her curse, a threat to her life. She had suffered so much for it—God knows how much suffering was yet in store... With a sad sigh, she turned the mirror towards the wall. She recalled...

She had decided to commit suicide that night. Reaching the bank of the raging, fuming, rumbling river she had stood on a steep rock. Far away in the hollows of the deep dark woods, a light had flickered in the ruins of the water mill. She had looked on unblinking. None could she trust. Relatives and clansmen, all were hungry wolves. The village men, all gutless. Tejuva had dragged her away before the very eyes of her husband, but he had looked on—as though he had been turned into a stone. How could one spend an entire lifetime with such an impotent being? Tejuva would rape her every day before his very eyes... She had been filled with an overpowering hatred.

She did not know how long she had stood still like a stone statue. A sound like a child's wail coming from a lonely dark hut, somewhere amidst the apple trees beyond, had penetrated her thoughts. A current had raced through her whole body. Kunnu's innocent, sad countenance swan before her eyes. What would become of him should she die? Would her demented husband take care of their son, or would he too suffer at the hands of his murderous granduncle and aunt?

"No! Oh no!" She had sobbed. Something had turned within her. Staring at the flicker of light far away she had run towards it like a woman possessed. The thin wrap covering her body in name only, had fluttered in the wind, but she had run on uncaring. How she had reached the other bank, she did not know. Drenched in the chilled water, shivering and panting, she had come to stand like a pillar before the door of the water mill. Water ran down in rivulets all over her body, her hair was a mess...

Khushal had come to the water mill that night, alone, to grind grain. He had sat dozing by the fire in a corner. The sound of the grinding of grains mingled with the noise of the river roaring outside. The water fell in a thick stream onto the heavy stone of the water wheel, rotating it at full speed. A large wooden funnel, grey with grime, hung from a rope tied to the roof and from it the grain fell into the hollow of the grinder. Khushal had stayed awake to change the lot of grain otherwise he would have fallen fast asleep, snug beneath the canopy of his blanket. There was 'manduva' to grind after the wheat. The 'manduva' was to be mixed with dried lumps of 'gethi'[31] which he had brought tied in a bundle from home and then ground, so that the flour would not be crumbly but would knead into a smooth dough.

He had been about to change the lot of grain when he had been startled to find the half-naked form of a woman standing at the door. She seemed scared out of her wits. His eyes were bulged in fear and he was bathed in sweat even in the freezing cold.

The cremation ground was nearby... O God! Was it a ghost or a witch? His face had gone white.

"W-wh-who?" he had screamed, trembling with fear.

Gomti was unnerved at seeing him so scared.

"I-I, be f-from L-Lad-Ladhaun", she stammered.

"Then why are you standing there like a ghost?" Khushal asked sharply.

Gomti was scared, "W-wanted to jump into the river, but...I am most unfortunate."

"O, my wretched fate!" Burying her face in her palm she broke into heart-rending sobs.

It had not taken long for Khushal to comprehend that the woman was a hapless victim of sad fate. Beckoning her to come near the fire, he had covered her with his blanket.

Gomti's tale of woes had moved him.

"Why do you want to die? Only they stand to gain by your death—why do you forget this?"

"What can I do? Who does not want to live? But all of them are after my life. I have a small child and for his sake alone I cannot die. Life will not ebb out of me, because he needs me..."

---

31. 'Gethi' - A sticky root

Khushal consoled her. Stroking her gently he said, "Crazy woman, what is to be gained by dying? Come with me to my house. I will give you shelter. I am of your caste and clan—from Sor, having settled in the farmland of Narsing Danda."

Gomti expressed no reaction to his proposal. She stood staring at the dying embers...

When Khushal had taken her hand she did not resist. In the dark of the night, she had fallen in step behind him—following like a cow led by the rope.

Khushalram had two other wives, both childless. He hungered for the joy of fatherhood. This was the ulterior motive besides Gomti's comely figure and dazzling beauty. An offspring was needed to perform the last rites at the time of his death. Without one there was no hope of 'sadgati'[32]. Just that.

Seeing this beautiful new intruder into their domain, at that early hours Khushal's two wives fumed, but Khushal's threatening looks cowed them into silence. Their barrenness was Khushal's strongest moral armour. So many well-wishers, within the family and outside had hinted many a time that he should marry again. Who knows he might still be blessed with offspring to carry on the family's name.

Khushal changed with Gomti's coming... He trimmed the bushy moustaches dropping over his lips and started wearing clothes with care. Entering the house, he would straighten his sagging shoulders and walk upright. He used to drink crude liquor; he now started getting betelnuts to chew from Khetikhan. Though above forty, he still had a powerful build.

---

32. 'Sadgati' - The soul merging with its creator.

There was a milch buffalo in his cattle pen and his own oxen. During the last two or three years, Budhanand Pandit's companionship had proved rewarding. The same Khushia who remained half-fed for three days in a week, now ate full meals thrice a day.

He would sling the Pandit's torn bag over his shoulder and follow him on his trips to the Nepal border a few times; and there would be enough to eat the whole year round.

The 'black gold' kept him in comfort. People talked; but who cared? Everyone was envious of his well-being, what else?

ELEVEN

Khushal breathed a sigh of relief, when, after paying Gomti's price, all those who had collected left for their homes. The guests for the ceremony also left by the evening. Khushalram's worries were over, his path was clear.

After the evening meal when Gomti came into his room, he showed her the 'panchayatnama' and said, "Those shroud-snatchers fleeced me of four hundred rupees!"

"How much is that?" Gomti was curious.

"Twenty times twenty rupees!" Gomti was amazed and wondered, "O my Ija!.. and you handed them so many rupees?"

"What else could I do? Those messengers of death would have dragged you away and treated you like a dog."

Gomti looked at Khushal with gratitude, "Hai! How will you pay back such a big loan?"

Khushal guffawed loudly, "To hell with the loan, woman! Do you take me for such a pauper?"

Pulling her to him, he bent over to look into her large blue eyes, "For you, even a lakh is nothing!"

Gomti smiled and Khushal took her into his arms.

He had been hungering for this pleasure all the while. After bringing her from the water mill, he led her to the lonely animal enclosure below for one or two nights, and tried to make love to her, but Gomti rebelled like an unbroken mare.

"I beg of you, do not try to do anything like this till it is decided whether or not I am to live in your house..."

He tried to assure her, "I give you my word that I will pay your price when the time comes."

"No, no. I am not like the others. When I have to live with you all my life, can you not wait for a few days?"

Khushal had given in to her wish and settling her clothes, which he had pulled off playfully, had gone up. Gomti spread her bedding near his two wives and went to sleep.

Today, Khushal was impatient, having paid in cash for making Gomti his very own. He instructed his eldest wife to spread his bedding separately in the box-room.

A kerosene lamp glowed in a niche in the wall, spewing a good deal of smoke.

"You have no complaint now...?"

Gomti smiled again, "Put out the lamp, I feel shy in this light...!"

Khushal laughed aloud, as was his habit.

"Even a virgin does not make all this fuss...!"

Gomti's fair face turned vermillion...

Khushal caught Gomti's nose between two fingers, "A nosering would sit pretty on this, with big, red flowerets! Will you wear it if I bring one for you?"

Gomti closed her eyes, overwhelmed with gratitude, and laughed...

"Your teeth are pretty and white like the seeds of a raw pomegranate, O Gomti! Let us see how sharp these are!"

Khushal put his little finger between her teeth—

Gomti bit it lightly.

Khushal was not satisfied. He coaxed, "Arre, this is not the way to bite—!"

"Then how?"

Khushal took Gomti's finger between his teeth and bit it so sharply that she hissed in pain, "O, Ma! What are you doing?"

Both of them were unaware that a streak of light through a chink in the door pierced the darkness in the next room.

Usually both the wives fell asleep and snored as soon as their heads hit the pillows, tired after the day's toil—but that day their sleep had vanished. God knew where! Both had fixed their gaze on the streak of light, their shivering bodies were all ears. They were trying to piece together the muffled, broken whispers, drawing their different meanings. They were filled with nostalgia for those days, when they too entered the inner box-room like this—they too had been beautiful then, bubbling over with the same youth!

The middle one could contain herself no longer, and sitting up in bed she put her ear to the chink in the door and tried to listen—

"I had brought some oranges from Sipti-Simad yesterday. Did the elder one give you?"

"Yes, she did—"

"She told me that you did not eat them, that you hid them for someone...!"

"Of course I ate them, right before everyone, sitting in the courtyard in the sun..."

"No, no, the eldest never lies. You must have hidden them somewhere."

"Where can they be hidden?"

"Shall I show you?"

"Yes—yes!"

Engaging Gomti in the banter, Khushal fiddled with the buttons of Gomti's 'angdi'. Pretending to feel something at last, he chuckled, "You thief! Shall I show you...?"

Gomti leapt up giggling. He gathered her in his arms, engulfing her in his embrace...

Her eyelids drooped; a sweet languor swept over her. Suddenly she noticed. Reaching out she snuffed the lamp and the chink of light vanished.

Neck-deep in gratitude, Gomti cast a spell over Khushal. To him, her willing surrender was the first wonderful experience of its kind, and seemed to drown him in its mysterious depths...

Khushal had to leave for work early the next morning. He left his bed at the crack of dawn, but Gomti lay in deep sleep till late.

The middle one went into the room, and opening the window, just a little, to let in the light; she looked at her... Gomti lay snoring in bed, her clothes dishevelled. Her thighs shapely as the banana trunk, two high mounds rising and falling with each breath, the fair wrists covered with so many green and red bangles which Khushal had slipped on the night before.

"This hussy will now rule the household!"

Sighing deeply the middle wife closed the door, and went out.

Despite the comforts, Gomti was not happy. Restive each moment of the day and night, she felt depressed in solitude. Khushal humoured her in every way, not letting her want for anything. She herself tried to forget everything, but could not, she was cursed...

Khushal's other two wives were inwardly jealous of her, but remained honey-sweet for all to see. They feared that if they say anything to her wilful Khushal would shake the soot down from the ceiling.

It was not so much Gomti's dazzling beauty that stung them, but their own barrenness. The blot was on them. Khushal had to get one off-spring to carry on his name. Therefore, he had to bring home another woman. What did it if the woman was Gomti?

A glassful of milk would remind Gomti of Kunnu. So much to eat here and none to feast on it...There he would be starving, looking hungrily at the neighbourhood children eating...and be chased away like a dog...

Durali was a daughter from the village Ladhaun, and had come only the day before. She addressed Gomti as 'Bojyu[33] 'by the old relationship. She had been telling Gomti, "Piram-Da has gone very weak now. Kaliya-Ka keeps him toiling all day, chiding him for the slightest fault, as he would a young lad. Poor Kunuva has been given the goats to take care of. Shivering in the cold he takes them grazing and roams the barren mountainside the whole day long."

33. 'Bojyu' - Brother's wife

TWELVE

"Why do you remain so sad...?" One day when Khushal asked, Gomti had not been able to answer.

"Anything here that makes you unhappy or uncomfortable?"

"N-no"

"Does the elder one or the middle one say anything unpleasant to you...?"

"N-no."

"Anything against me?"

"How could you think that way?"

"Then what is the matter? Say something." When Khushal spoke gruffly like this, Gomti burst into sobs and ran into the next room.

Seeing Khushal unusually happy one night, she chose an intimate moment to implore him.

"Can I say something...?"

"Yes, yes!"

"You will not take it otherwise?"

Khushal shook his head, "No."

"...Can Kunnu not come here...? I will feel happier and he could do some of our work here. He could take the buffalo to pasture in the fallow fields!"

Khushal was not prepared for this kind of a request at such a time. Taken aback, he pondered for a while, then looking at Gomti, he said, "How can it be so? Would it look nice, his coming here? I will not be able to tolerate someone coming between the two of us. Besides, Kaliya had taken from me in writing at the time of the settlement, that the child will stay with the father. Tell me, how can I bring him here now?"

"..."

"You do not know, even if I were to say yes, even if there had been nothing on paper, do you think Kaliya would let him come here? Who will serve that swine there? I know that toothless rascal inside out..."

Seeing Gomti's woebegone face, Khushal took pity.

Caressing her, he consoled, "Why be unhappy for what was left behind, for what is over now? Tell me, what happiness did you receive from that mad husband of yams, who was as good as dead? As for the child, 'Siddhanarsing Baba's[34] blessings be showered upon you. You will have one of your own here, very soon. You will have a child, No?"

How was Gomti to pour out her heart's sorrow? Should she now forsake the same child for whom she had not been able to commit suicide the other day?

About two months later, Durali took her two children and younger sister-in-law with her to her parents' home for the naming ceremony of her brother. Gomti quietly sent a half-moon of jaggery, and a handful of parched soybean and beaten rice, all stitched up in a little bag, for Kunnu.

"Tell him, your mother has sent these."

---

34. 'Siddhanarsing Baba' - Diety of the village

She remembered to send along an old torn shirt of Khushal—for Pirma. What would he be wearing in the biting cold?

Durali had promised to return within five or six days, but she came back a full month later.

Gomti had gone to fetch water from the spring, and it was there that she met Durali by chance.

"You were away a long time, Duru..."

"What could I do, Bojyu? The little one fell ill as soon as I got there..."

"How is he now?"

"We cannot understand it. Gangatuva said that 'Manjhali'[35] Kaki's ghost has come upon him; it has to be appeased. We will sacrifice a goat on the sixteenth day of this month, at the shrine of the God of 'Kail Bakariya'."

Gomti paused before asking, "Did Kunnu meet you?"

"Of course, Bojyu, I did see him. He passed our front yard each time he took the goats to graze. I gave him the things you sent..."

"Did he say anything?"

"Nothing. He was overjoyed to see the little bag. Snatched it like a monkey, and started devouring with both his hands...?"

"Anything else...?"

"As he ate, I asked him if he remembered his mother. Tears welled up in his eyes. He picked up the bag and ran away."

Hearing this Gomti's heart was pierced with a shaft of pain. Her face clouded over with sorrow. She stood lost in

35. 'Manjhali' - Middle one

thought, then seemed to remember something. Distractedly she asked, "Did he have anything on his body, Duru? This year it is freezing cold, a torturous winter..."

"He had tucked on Pirma-Da's old, torn 'kurta' over his own. The skin of his hands and feet was chapped from the cold. Blood seeped through the cracks...the heartless brutes send him out to the jungle, even in this weather—to bring the bark of the pine and cedar for lighting their fires."

Durali returned with her water pot filled. Gomti sat motionless. holding her copper pitcher...

THIRTEEN

Winter had begun, snow would soon be falling. The sharp winds seemed to grate the skin. The fields, the bams, the waterflows, all were covered overnight with thick layers of ice, transparent like sheets of glass. Half-naked children, shivering in the cold, would hack away at the ice lumps to suck them, away from the eyes of their parents. Such a thick, white frost descended upon the cool dense forests, that it seemed as though snow had fallen. It became nearly impossible to walk barefoot through the dark valleys and dense forests. The hands and feet quickly turned blue and numb with the cold.

The children went around collecting dried pine cones by the sackfuls for burning at home. Entire settlements lay vacated, caravans of people along with their families, their cattle and essential belongings, descending on foot to the 'tarai' plains at the foothills, to escape the cold and savour the sunshine below. They would find work through the winter and the wages earned would ensure rice for their bellies.

Khushal was planning to go with Pandit Budhanand to Doti in Nepal when he learnt that a bear had caught the Pandit as he was crossing the dense forests of Khinyali Birgul surrounding the high mountains. As the Pandit stooped to drink water, a giant black bear emerged from behind the 'kaphal' trees, growling. He heard its 'gr-r-r, gr-r!', but before the Pandit could rise, the beast clasped him in a fierce embrace. They struggled for a long time.

Giving its coat of long, needle-sharp, black hair a vigorous shake, the bear turned towards the forests of cedar and rolled out of sight.

By then the Pandit had been badly wounded. The bear had mauled his arms, legs and face.

Somehow he had dragged himself and reached the village Birgul by nightfall. The people had no hope of his survival and putting him on a 'dandi'[36], they rushed him overnight to the Mayawati Hospital.

Khushal was ridden with worry. What if the Pandit died?

What would become of their 'trade'? Would he be reduced to the same hand-to-mouth existence? The pair of oxen would have to go. His status would be reduced from Khushalram, the craftsman, to Khushia the ironsmith. The Pandit must be dragged out of the jaws of death, and with this in mind, Khushal set out for Mayawati the same evening to nurse the Pandit back to health. The Pandit had brought him prosperity and comfort. He did not want to back out of the moral obligation to be with him in this hour of need.

The sun shone after a long time. Gomti sat in the courtyard spreading out her wet hair to dry in the sun when she saw Durali's daughter before her, "Thul Ija, my Ija calls you."

"What for, my little bird?"

"How should I know? Go, ask her!" and the little girl skipped away.

---

36. 'Dandi' - Carrier on foot

Rinsing her hair free of the water, Gomti coiled her tresses and covering her head with her 'pichhaudi' she went over to Durali' s house where she saw Khimu-Ka smoking tobacco in the front yard. Gomti pulled down her head-cover to cover her face also and bent at his feet to offer her respects. Khimu-Ka extended his right hand in blessing.

"How are you, daughter-in-law?" Khimu-Ka coughed out the smoke.

"As well as can be—"

"—"

"Would all be well back home?" Gomti was anxious to know.

"Yes, all is well—" he continued to draw on the tobacco. There was a long silence.

Gomti asked, "How did you come so suddenly, 'Sasur Jyu'[37]?"

"Just like that, daughter-in-law," Khimu-Ka inhaled deeply..."Bought a goat from Kanaan village. Thought that I should look up Durali on my way. Son-in-law minds very much that I do not come here, what to do?"

Silence descended again. Resting the 'chillum' against the wall, he said thoughtfully, "Our Pirmuwa is in a poor state..." a deep sigh escaped him.

"Kaliya's progeny will suffer in hell for tormenting his nephew and his child. Some money came from the front, in settlement of Debiya's accounts. They say that the rascal devoured even that money... Patwari Jyu came to the village on the twenty-sixth day of the last month and took Kaliya to task. It is heard that before his death Debiya had written to the government that his family members

37. 'Sasur Jyu' - Father-in-law

were being exploited. He was away on the front and in his absence there was none to protect them back home. Should he die on the front, what would become of them?"

Saying this Khimu-Ka faltered. His vacant eyes seemed to search for something, "If our Debiya were alive today, this black-hearted rascal Kaliya would not be so bold. It is said that before returning to the front, Debiya had told Gumansingh, the shop owner in Pokhari that if ever Kaliya-Ka raises his hands against his brother's family again, Debiya would shoot Kaliya's family one by one; let him be hanged for it if he would... The unfortunate boy is gone, what can be done now? Kaliya fears none now. That pariah pup of his, Tejuva, acts as village chief, beating up whosoever he wishes to. The 'panch' and 'sarpanch' are all in his pocket... He makes hooch in the village and serves it openly. These rascals have corrupted the entire village, what to do?"

Short in stature and thin, poor Khimu-Ka became worked up with rage, relating all this.

"The day before yesterday they raised their hands on our Harali. Lachhiya was not at home that day, or there would have been bloodshed."

Gomti stood motionless, hearing it all, her head bent.

"You also sit down, Bojyu," Durali said, but Gomti remained standing, eyes downcast.

"Daughter-in-law," Khimu-Ka addressed her, "I called you here to suggest that you should call Kunuwa here, otherwise his plight will be the same as his father's. He is given the dog's share to eat, and that too not enough. He is all bones—our heart pierces to see him thus..."

Gomti bit hard on her lower lip and sat down limply on the mud floor, beside the half wall—

"You do something, Sasur Jyu." Gomti folded her hands in a tearful plea, "I cannot think of anything. What should I do, why have I been so ill-fated...?"

Durali brought a tall glassful of milky tea flavoured with fenugreek seeds and black peppercorns. Offering a tiny lump of moist jaggery, she said, "Take this, Bojyu."

Gomti clasped the glass of hot tea, but could not sip it. She would bring the glass to her lips, then put it away, but Khimu-Ka drank in loud slurps, licking the moist jaggery, stuck to a finger, with each sip[38]—

Soon he had finished half a glass. Their mouths let escape vapour which mingled with the steam that rose from the tea glasses.

"Makes hooch in the jungle, that blot on a fair name! If someone should report it, both father and son will get a life-term..." Putting the empty glass on the half-wall, Khimu-Ka rose quickly. Throwing the end of his coarse woollen wrap over one shoulder he set out, pulling the bleating goat by its rope.

Suddenly dense black clouds came hovering from the side of Sipti-Simad. How would he reach Ladhaun in time if it started to rain? It would be night by the time he reaches Khetikhan.

Khushal was home from Mayawati, for a day. At night Gomti said to him, "Kaliya makes hooch on the sly, right in the middle of the forest—Khimu-Ka was saying today. If someone reported to the government, they are sure to be behind bars!" Gomti gave his face a searching look, awaiting a reaction.

---

38. In order to make do with the minimum of sweetner in a beverage.

Khushal was taken aback by this unexpected, unpleasant topic at such a time.

"Kaliya scoundrel can go behind bars or be hanged, how should it concern you?" Khushal cracked down upon her, "Why are you tormenting yourself for them? A thousand times I have said, do not think of that place and those people but you seem to have taken leave of your senses. The day you came here, that very day Kaliya, Pirma, Kunuva—all died for you! Damn them all, why do you bring up their names now? This angers me."

Gomti froze into silence.

She had hoped that since Khushal knew a number of people, and since the 'patwari' and the forest guard listened to him, if he were to file a complaint, Kaliya and Tejuva would be punished for their sins. Hearing Khushal's brusque reply she watched him helplessly, open-mouthed.

She had everything here but peace of mind. Khushal did not let her want for anything of any kind. Borrowing a little from here and there, he had got a few ornaments made for her, besides three or four sets of clothes. There was no dearth of food, yet she pined...

If food and clothing was what she hankered for, she could have got it from anyone. Where does one not get food in return for one's body? But whenever had she so desired?

She was filled with a strange depression. She began to feel that perhaps, even here, there was no riddance from sorrow and pain.

FOURTEEN

Khushal had not been able to set out for Doti-Nepal this year with Pandit Budhanand for the usual 'trade'. Pandit Budhanand had returned from the hospital after a full two months, completely unrecognisable. His jaw seemed merged with the nose; there was a gaping hole, the size of a walnut, where the right eye had been. The bear had gouged it out and had clawed at him badly in so many places, that he made a fearsome sight. The children would take fright and flee at the sight of him.

He still wanted to salvage his luck. Being in no state to venture out to Doti-Nepal anymore, he had found a way out here, back home. He planned to roam the villages to buy and collect black sticks of hashish and opium. In this too his closest associate would be Khushal.

Unfortunately, this venture did not thrive. Eight or nine months of roaming brought nothing in hand. Budhanand thought of a new plan—to rear goats.

The Pandit would invest and Khushal would be responsible for rearing and selling the animals. The income would be shared equally. Pandit Budhanand was a 'brahmin', hence he could not take up goat trading—what would the people say? So he cleverly roped in Khushal.

In the first lot came eleven goats and two he-goats. Khushal built a hut-like enclosure of grass and straw, in front of his house. The crisis was over, he was happy again.

It was the time of the 'Phooldol' fair near Rikheshwar in Lohaghat. Many from the village were preparing to go. Khushal asked Gomti too, but she was not keen.

"I do not feel like it."

"You are a crazy woman!" Khushal said, "I'll buy you some clothes. You could have your fill of milk and 'jalebi', and bring home some coconut and crystal-sugar to eat. Your days of fun and good eating have just begun—come on!" Khushal laughed aloud. Gomti went reluctantly. Some relatives from the Kalkot side were also expected at the fair. Khushal wished to show her off; if she went all decked up, it would add to his prestige. There would be talk of his prosperity among his brethren, and in the community. With this in mind, Khushal ordered her to don the colourful clothes and adorn herself with the anklets, bracelets and necklaces, which he had bought from the Tanakpur market. Gomti was weighed down with the burden of her own adornments.

Khushal spent liberally in the fair. He bought braids for Gomti, bangles, big red 'bindis'; gaudy silk scarves, all for her.

It was the remainder of the 'trade' profit perhaps; which Khushal was spending so lavishly. He was not content with all that he had bought for Gomti. Before returning home in the evening he got a packetful of sweetmeats. Settling Gomti beside the other women from the village, near the bus stop, he went up to the patwari's camp for some urgent work. There was a crowd of people returning from the fair. The problem was that if only one bus was to go up to Khetikhan, how would so many passengers be accommodated?

"O Bojyu, one can hardly recognise you! So many ornaments?" It was Harali from Ladhaun, Khimu-Ka's younger daughter, and by that relationship, she addressed Gomti as Bojyu. She touched the ornaments in wonder.

"What is the weight of these earrings, ho? Where did you get these anklets made? This 'pichhaudi' with fine silky piping all around becomes you well—like the 'buronj' flower! Shiny and pretty!"

Gomti felt shy, unable to speak. Taking Harali a little away from the crowd, she gave her the packet of sweets, "Give this to my Kunnu."

There and then Gomti bought a whistle and a pipe, and tucked it in the pocket of Harali's 'angdi', "Do not forget, ho..." Gomti's voice quivered.

Haltingly she asked, "How is your brother?"

"You mean Pirma-Da?"

"Yes! Yes!"

"Oh! Do you not know Bojyu? Do not tell anyone. When Patwari Jyu raided Kaliya-Ka's hooch outfit, it was Pirma-Da who got nabbed. The rest had already slipped away. Handcuffed, he was brought to Lohaghat the day before. They say he is in the lock-up now." Harali whispered in one breath.

Soon after, Chinta came. "I have given the 'bidi' to Pirma-Da. He is in the lock-up nearby, poor fellow. Someone commits the crime, and someone else suffers for it..."

The lock-up was near the bus stop. Its black slated roof was clearly visible below the road, amongst the cedar trees. Gomti gazed at it then throwing a wary glance around her, she moved away stealthily, holding Harali's hand, leaving the big bundle of purchases with the women sitting beside her.

The lock-up was below the road, on a slight slope. The large iron bars were clearly visible from the road above. The wet earth being slippery, Gomti descended cautiously.

Her anxious gaze searched for something in the dark cell surrounded by tall iron bars.

Just then a shadow moved away.

With his back to the door on the riverside, Pirma was peeping outside. Clad in rags, his chin resting on his knees, his eyes filled with a vacant gaze. A small patch of faint yellow sunshine, filtering through the iron bars lay scattered near his feet. Emaciated body, dully, filmy eyes, bent back ...

Holding the cold iron bars with both her hands, Gomti looked at the skeleton before her.

The stub of a burnt-out 'bidi' was held between the two fingers of his right hand. Looking at Gomti who was standing right before him, he seemed to be staring through her.

She looked at him, unblinking, with tear-filled eyes.

"Why don't say, you haven't committed any crime, you haven't." Gomti wanted to shriek out but the words eddied and formed a lump in her throat.

"O Bojyu, the motor has come. Aren't you coming, ho?" Harali beckoned from above. Gomti came out of her trance.

There was some crystal-sugar, wrapped in paper, tucked inside the pocket of her 'angdi'. Gomti put her hands between the bars and dropped it in front. Taking out some notes, and some coins too from the pocket, she threw it all inside the cell.

"—Might come in useful for 'bidi' and tobacco sometime!"

But Pirma did not pick them up from the floor. He stared queerly at the things strewn before him, unmoving.

◎◎◎

“Where had you gone?” Khushal stood holding the bus ticket.

“Just nearby...”

“Arre? Why are you weeping?” Khushal asked in surprise.

Gomti forced a laugh.

“How am I weeping? I am laughing...!” and she snuggled close to Khushal.

Hiding her inner anguish, Gomti did not falter in her duties towards Khushal. Whatever he wanted, she did dutifully, unquestioningly. Never did she open her mouth in reply, obeying him with her head bowed. Pledged to be with him in life, and in death, she was a thorn in the flesh for Khushal’s other two wives, who remained ignored constantly. Gomti was with him day and night, the household keys were in her possession.

Lugging the pine logs for the goat enclosure, the elder one threw a tantrum one day, “Go, you pamper her beauty, you do not care further who toils for you. So besotted with her you are. We should labour in the fields and she should rule the household just sitting idle and eating? Laden with juicy fruits, is she?”

“Someone will remain in the house to cook the meals.”

“Aha, yes, yes! She will remain in the house, who else? If she does not stay back at home, how will she pamper her previous husband? How will she filch your clothes and send them to him? How will she pass on to her son the lumps of jaggery and bagfuls of 'chiwda'[39] and parched soybean? And you, how will you escort her to Lohaghat to meet her previous husband? If I am lying, then ask Durali! Call Khimli! When she went to the 'Phooldol' fair, she sneaked off to meet him in the lock-up. She sheds tears for him the whole day long, the wretch. If she pines for him so, why does she not go and blacken her face with him? The witch has come as a curse to our house..."

Khushal had remained silent then, but later when others too mentioned it, he was filled with rancour, the snakes of suspicion coiling around his heart had sharp fangs. All this after doing so much for her? Had the wretch leapt into the river and drowned, he would not have earned such ill-fame, nor would he have had to pay her price.

He remained disturbed the whole day and gulping down a large mouthful of liquor, he passed out. Gomti finished up the kitchen work and reached the room, only to find it plunged in darkness. The oil lamp had not been lighted. She ignited a strip of bark from the cooking fire and lighted the room.

Awakening Khushal, she handed him a glassful of hot milk, "What? A sleep even before nightfall? Caught a chill? Fever?"

Khushal remained silent, holding the glass. Wrapping his cold fingers around the hot metal tumbler to warm them, he stared at Gomti.

His eyes were bloodshot, his face grey with pallor. Fixing her with a crooked stare, he taunted, "Missing your son too much? Yearning for him, no?"

Gomti looked wordlessly at Khushal, he had never put such a question before. Why, then, this sudden curiosity today?

---

39. 'Chiwda' - Beaten rice

"I am asking something—speak up"

"Y-yes, sometimes," she nodded.

"You miss Piramuva too?"

Gomti bowed her head.

"Want to go back to him?"

Gomti knew not what to say. She scratched the clay and cow-dung-smeared earthen floor with her toe-nail.

Khushal was worked up. He said, a little louder, "I ask, do you want to go back to them?"

"Yes, with your permission—!" Gomti could contain herself no longer and flung herself at his feet, "My heart is not happy here, truly. I want to go and see my Kunuwa once. I heard he is very ill...all bones..."

"Then why don't you stay with them?" Khushal said lost in thought.

Hearing this Gomti was overwhelmed with gratitude. Looking up with tear-filled eyes, she whispered, "If you say so...! The worst that could happen would be that Tejuva will slaughter us all. If I die with them even, I will have no regrets..."

Khushal was on edge, his control snapped. Convulsed with anger he looked at her in fury. Landing a violent kick on her bosom, he burst out, "Bitch! Wretch! If you want to die with them, then why did you play this drama? Why did you come here? Why did you not die there? Were you a woman of virtue, you would have stuck by them, not roamed from door to door like a bitch..."

Gomti huddled up on the bed.

What on earth had overcome Khushal? He himself had raised the topic and she had replied in all earnestness and simplicity...Her mind was in turmoil. She suffered not from the blow but another kind of anguish...

"How can you think of going from here, say?" Khushal roared. "The compensation was deposited by me. I paid the amount with a loan of four hundred rupees. Pay back your father's debt, then think of crossing this threshold. I too will see how you go back to that rogue, Piramuwa. I will drag you from there, slut! You must be in search of a new lover. I know your cunning..." Gomti reeled with shock... She did not return to his bed, but sat huddled in one corner, shivering.

Memories of her past crept back...

The same had happened to her when she had been married for the first time in Chalees Patti, before her marriage to Pirma. She was twelve years old when she had first gone to her husband's home.

She had barely broken her milk teeth, being quite ignorant of the ways of the world. What is marriage? Why it is performed?

She did not know. She was delighted with so many pretty clothes though!

After finishing the evening meal, the widow of her husband's elder brother had led her by the hand to an inner room, and leaving her there she had come out and locked the door from outside.

Gomti had no father-in-law or mother-in-law, there were no sisters or brothers to her husband who had been living with this distantly related childless widow, his sister-in-law, for the last three years. But for the pressure from relatives, he would never have married.

Gomti was frightened in the dark room, then she heard footsteps. It did not take her long to guess that they were her husband's.

Holding her by the hand, he led her in the dark to his bed. What did she know about the husband-wife relationship? Blissfully ignorant, she crept silently into the warm bed. The day had been tiring, her eyelids were dropping with sleep. She had almost dozed when her newly wedded husband began running his hands all over her, whispering endearments. Gathering her in a passionate embrace, he pressed her to him. Gomti felt suffocated. She bore it all mutely up to a limit. But when her husband's lovemaking crossed the limit, the girl in her broke into a sweat. When the pain became unbearable, she screamed. Her husband carried on showing his brutal strength and Gomti's screams became louder and louder.

Her husband was overwhelmed with a sudden disgust; losing all patience he dealt a severe blow on Gomti's bare back and flung her aside like a worm.

Gomti was huddled into a heap, sobbing, when the outer bolt of the door was lifted and her sister-in-law stormed into the dark room, "O, Devar Jyu, you will not be able to tackle her all by yourself. I will set her right." Saying this she drafted Gomti back to her husband's bed. With his help, she clamped down Gomti's knees with both her sturdy feet and twisted her wrists, "Dare to whimper now...!"

Her husband pressed his palm so heavily over her mouth that Gomti was not able to cry out.

Sometime later she rolled over to one side in a helpless state, bathed in sweat.

She moaned with unbearable pain, her whole body shaking like a leaf. Her sister-in-law dragged her out of the room and returning to it she bolted the door from inside. Gomti lay in a strange stupor, shivering till the morning, all alone.

That was the first time she had been raped by her own husband...

She had felt dejected the same way as she did today...

Today, too, something similar was being done but in a different manner. When Khushal flung her out of the room, both the other wives went inside together at once and bolted the door from inside...The next morning Gomti's face lost all its colour. When she returned with the pitchers of water, Khushal's two wives took advantage of his absence and snatched away the ornaments and the household keys.

Gomti became like a nun. She worked outside the whole day and night, filling water, bringing the fodder from the jungle, and chopping wood. She had to clean the enclosure for the cattle and goats. At night she slept on a tattered rug on the verandah.

FIFTEEN

"Your Ija is seriously ill, she has called you to see her face for the last time." The horseman, going to Champavat on a court errand, informed Gomti.

In this whole wide world, her mother's home was the only shelter where Gomti could take refuge in the darkness of the night or light of the day, without being questioned. She had never known what it was like to have a father, never known paternal love or care. What had her husbands given her? There was only her mother in whose lap she could bury her head and cry her heart out; before whom she could pour out all her inner anguish.

Starving herself, Gomti's mother would never forget to send something or the other to her daughter on festive occasions. Custom ordained that numerous gifts be sent to daughters on every festival—the 'diwali' sweets of sesame seed 'laddoos', and beaten rice before the onset of winter. From where did she procure all this to send for Gomti? She could barely eke out a living for herself. Even then she would scrape together something, a handful from her employer, from the brahmin, from the landlord, and make it all into a gift for Gomti.

If this refuge was gone what would be left for Gomti? Whose door would Gomti knock on in times of stress and need? Cleaning out the cattle enclosure, sweeping out the goatpen, Gomti was filled with sorrowful thoughts. She pondered over her mother's home for a few days...

Khushal had just returned from the village, the end of his coarse woollen wrap thrown carelessly over his shoulder. He sat resting beneath the dry grass roof of the cattle-shelter outside in the front yard. Gomti fetched him cool water to drink and his 'hukka' filled with tobacco.

Khushal puffed at the hukka, gazing intently at Gomti—the fair wrists are smudged with cow-dung. Her 'angdi' and 'pichhaudi' are soiled. The feet were smeared with cow-dung up to the ankles, her 'ghaghri' hitched high—the firm smooth calves dotted with grime—

Leaning against the pole of the shelter, Gomti stood nibbling a straw, "There is a message from my mother's home, she is seriously ill...Shall I give her up as dead also, just as I have given up Pirma and Kunuva? That's what you want. Or shall I go and see her face as she lies on her deathbed?" The words stuck in her throat.

A cool shiver ran down Khushal's spine. He stared unblinking at Gomti, her youthful figure still enveloped in the heady fragrance of youth. There were furrows beneath her dreamy blue eyes...

"Gomti, you have misunderstood me?"

Gomti whispered, "You meted out such treatment to me. What more could you do now...? Not content with raising your hands to me, you have got me beaten up by your other wives. I could have sought out anyone to live with, and could have got what I wanted, but that was not what I wished for. I would be, content in my small world of broken dreams, but people would not let me be...hounding me as if I were a bitch...!"

Gomti's eyes were flooded.

Khushal rose and gathered her in his arms, "Gomi, you have misunderstood me. I only wished that you should not think of others now, that is why I..."

"A mother should not think about her son? Am I a she-snake? Can I forget my own flesh and blood, born of my own womb? Do you take me for a woman of the road, whom you have bought for rupees twenty times twenty?" Gomti's nostrils quivered in anger.

Khushal had never seen Gomti like this. It took him by surprise. Her flushed face looked many times more beautiful.

Khushal took her to his room that night, but Gomti lay like a stone beside him, her body lifeless.

"My heart is not in it. Leave me. I want nothing now."

How could Khushal leave her untouched? He stroked her naked body far into the night. Not in his wildest imagination could he think of living without her.

"If your mother is ill then go to appease your anxiety. But do not go towards Ladhaun... Return by tomorrow no matter what happens..."

Gomti remained motionless.

"I will get you more clothes, I will have more ornaments fashioned for you."

Gomti set out to visit her ailing mother early next morning before sunrise.

The old woman's condition was unchanged, neither alive nor any signs of death setting her free from her physical agony. A mere skeleton lay on the bed of straw, the thin skin, like parchment, stretched over the bones. Gomti's maternal uncle's wife had arrived that very day from Bhaura village, to nurse her sister-in-law.

In the front yard, iron was being hammered into shape. A group of men sat talking around the fire, "Pirma will be out of jail soon. The case has gone to the court. When he has committed no crime why should he be punished?'

"What has punishment got to do with crime?"

"It may or may not, but he will be back soon, wait and see."

—The argument went on, but Gomti's eyes were following the movement of the sun. She had promised to return to Narsing Danda that very day. If she was not back by night a storm would be kicked up.

"Ija, I will come again...!" saying this she set out alone. Gomti's heart was heavy. Her feet would not move towards Narsing Danda. Ladhaun was clearly visible from the crest of the Piplati hills. The last rays of the setting sun took their last peep at the pine-clad hilltops.

—Kunnu would be minding the goats somewhere on these barren hilltops.

—Kaliya would be bullying Kunnu every day, dragging him by the ears like he would a pariah pup.

—Would there be any tatters left on his body? The hapless boy would be shivering naked in the cold!... How would he be feeling with his father in jail? Abandoned? Helpless...?

—Such anguish

—Such torture...

Gomti's head reeled. She sat down beside the narrow mountain trail, clutching her forehead.

When darkness fell, her feet staggered on, not towards Narsing Danda, but somewhere else, in a different direction.

SIXTEEN

When Gomti did not return even after three or four days, Khushal was worried. A messenger, sent to enquire from Gomti's mother, returned to say that she had left the place that very day before sunset.

She had not reached Ladhaun either.

Then?

Khushal rubbed his palms boiling with rage. He was gnawed with guilt that had she not been admonished and suppressed as she had been, she would probably not have run away. He put all the blame on the two wives who had not only removed Gomti's ornaments, but had also snatched away the household keys from her by force. She had been pushed into the verandah as if she were an eyesore.

Kaliya-Ka and Tejram had the last laugh. Whenever the topic came up they would recount over and over again, "We always said that the hussy was not of good character. It is heard that she has run away from Narsing Danda too. Khushia would be cursing his fate. She cannot stay in one place. Like the lioness who gets the taste of human flesh, so she had had a taste of lovers ... Who knows how many more she will devour...!"

Khimu-Ka's aged wife would beckon little Kunnu and give him a morsel of stale 'roti', or fling on his naked frame her children's worn garments.

"This unfortunate lad was born with the worst luck. An orphan—even with both parents alive. Who will share his sorrow?"

A simple affectionate soul, she would be overwhelmed with pity.

"Kunuwa, whenever you go hungry, slip away quietly and come hither, son! To me, you are just like my Patiya..."

Some said that Gomti had gone down to the foothills. Rudiya had seen her in Pansing's cart May be a lorry driver had carried her off.

Some thought that she could be dead too—to be rid of sorrow...

◎◎◎

Gomti roamed Bhingrada and the lower hills for some months. Taking temporary refuge with some relatives on her mother's side, she descended to the 'tarai' plains with their families when winter set in. She would pound paddy for someone, chop bamboo for someone's hut, carry bricks and mortar for a house being built, cut grass on someone's farm—the work would provide her two 'rods', surely.

Gomti was faced with a bigger problem. She would have to save each pie to scrape together enough to pay back Khushal's compensation money so as to be able to return to Ladhaun. Her heart was wrenched with longing to be with her ailing husband and the little lamb—her son.

—If they were fated to perish, then perish they would, but the three of them would die together. She could be reconciled no more, at any cost, to leaving them in the lair of those two-legged beasts!

Many poor women laboured with their families in the fertile plains of 'tarai'[40], to earn an extra mouthful of rice. Gomti became one of them.

---

40. 'Tarai' - The rich fertile land at the foothills of Kumaon.

Gomti roamed the cattle enclosures of Sainapani, Dogadi for some time, then stayed with some relatives in Khatima. The dense forests of 'tarai' were being cleared to make way for new farms. Cheap labour was much in demand for the forest clearing campaign. Gomti joined the human herds, working day and night, digging out the roots of the felled trees. The hollows had to be packed with earth and evened out, for tractors to go over the patches without any obstacles.

Blisters covered her hands which became raw from slinging the spade and axe. There were dark circles beneath her eyes. Gomti did not care whether it was day or night, but worked like a woman possessed.

After two or three months of backbreaking labour, she had managed to save only rupees four times twenty! She needed twenty times twenty! To save this much money seemed to her as formidable as scaling the Panchchuli peak. She was desperate and unhappy.

"This woman works hard", Lala Tirpan Lal would puff out his hollow cheeks, amazed to see her work thus.

"Fells the tallest trees with quick strikes of the axe..."

Tirpan Lal had a flour mill in Khatima 'mandi', managed by his sons. From time to time he took forest contracts to supply wood for construction projects. Along with all this, he had cut a large farm, far away from the city, near Banbasa, and for the past few years, a portion of the farm was under sugarcane cultivation. He now planned to clear the rest of the farm to cultivate paddy.

A tubewell had been installed. A thatched roof on the southern tip of the farm became the labourers' temporary abode. There were more farms adjacent to this one, owned by people like Tirpan Lal, yielding two plentiful crops each year. Tirpan Lal was now eager that the same lush greenery should flood his farm too! The Goddess of wealth "Laxmi' would descend not only upon his trade now, but on his farm too, or so he imagined. That is why the work on his farm was put on a war footing.

Pleased with Gomti's work, Lala Tirpan Lal had raised her wages to equal a male labourer's earnings. If she expected more, he would quietly slip an extra note along with her wages and would guffaw for no rhyme or reason.

Gomti did not know how to count. She would save each pie of her earnings, knotting it up in a dirty rag for safekeeping.

Many a time, on the pretext of some work or the other, the Lala called Gomti on the quiet, and tried to lure her with his offer to instal her permanently on the farm; but Gomti retorted angrily, "We may be in need Lala, but we are not of that sort..."

"Ho-ho-ho!" the Lala would stroke his bald head and puff his hollow cheeks.

"We were not suggesting otherwise...anything wrong in working on a farm?"

Gomti would come away.

With the onset of summer, those who had descended the hills, turned to go back. The temporary settlements of straw huts gradually became deserted. After the Shivaratri[41] fast, even the sawyers engaged in sawing logs of wood to be used in construction projects scrambled towards home in crowded buses, their saws and bundles of their purchases of jaggery, clothing and grain slung over their shoulders. The caravans which had come down eagerly to the 'tarai' plains in winter were now impatient to hurry back to the hills.

---

41. 'Shivaratri'- The fast of Lord Shiva

Lala Tirpan Lal settled the accounts of the labourers. Hand-ing Gomti her wages, he did not forget to nudge her, "Would you listen? Beniram was saying that there is none to wait for you at home. Why do you not work here? As long as Tirpan Lal is here, you will be well off, indeed!"

Gomti gave him a withering look, "I have everyone in my family at home, Lala. E-v-e-r-y-o-n-e. Only for them have I been labouring thus. Binnam said that to humour you. Do not take me wrong, Lala, I am not that kind of a woman."

Chewing his thick and ugly lips the Lala chuckled slyly, "What did I say to you? Tell me! Anything wrong in working, is there?"

The poor family of a retired old soldier from Sor in Pithoragarh had stayed back on the Lala's farm last year. Besides the rations every month, the Lala gave them a few rupees every now and then. The women, men, old and young of the family toiled away on the farm, day and night, under the blazing hot sun and in the rain. This year their exodus to Banbasa had upset the Lala. A Sardarji's farm was adjacent to his own. It would be difficult to depend on the watchman of that farm. During the rainy season, there was every danger of the entire crop being trampled by wild elephants.

There was no dearth of available labour but the Lala was a miser. Every pie spent took his life. He had engaged an old woman to stay on the farm that summer. The woman had none to call her own back home in the hills, and she had decided to spend her remaining years on the Lala's farm. But she had cataract and was completely sightless in the dark.

All the workmen took their wages and prepared to take their families back by way of Chorgaliya. Gomti too tied up her belongings and joined the group.

After spending the night in Chorgaliya the group would begin their long trek back home. The first ascent would begin early, before daybreak. The mood all around was jubilant because after basking in the sun for two or three months, and having had their fill of rice they had also earned enough to be able to afford a puff of tobacco now and then. Their children would have clothes.

The sky was starlit; the air was not warm any more. The group had camped beneath a 'pipal' tree. Horses, cows, bullocks and goats were tied to pegs beneath the surrounding trees. Some 'dal' simmered in a vessel perched atop the fire lit between two bricks; a little rice cooked nearby.

Gomti had handed someone her share of the 'dal' and rice for cooking. But she could not swallow the food. Feigning a headache she slept.

The day had been tiring. After meals, the weary flopped on their beds. The fire nearby slowly died out. But Gomti's eyes were wide open. She had managed to scrape together only a few rupees after back-breaking labour. News of her return would soon reach Khushal. He would storm up with three or four persons to drag her back to the same hell... Pirma would do his rounds of the Jail. Kunuwa would forever be with the goat herd in someone else's employment. She would always live on the leavings of others. All would claw at her like so many vultures...

"Oh God," Gomti moaned...

All rose before daybreak for the trek back home. The cattle had been put forth on the onward journey while it was still night. Bundling up their belongings and tying them on the backs of bullocks and horses, everyone took a quick wash and set forth. The caravan kicked up a cloud of dust on the steep and muddy hill tracks. The little bells tied onto the necks of animals tinkled into the night. All were eager to cover as much distance as they could in the cool of the morning. The hills would become difficult to scale in the blazing sun.

Gomti too had picked up her bundles but her feet faltered. She lagged behind them all alone. A wild, murderous elephant had created terror in the area for the past few days. All moved in a crowd beating their 'thalis' and bells. There was even provision for lighting a fire if necessary.

By afternoon when they camped for meals, Gomti was nowhere in sight.

SEVENTEEN

"Lala, I want work." Gomti put down her bundle and wiped away the sweat.

Lala Tirpan Lal guffawed as was his habit.

"The whole farm is thine. What do you need to work for?"

"No, no Lala. You had wanted me to labour in the field!"

"Alright 'baba'! We told you before that the farm is yours! We knew that you would return. Tirpan Lal's hair has not turned white in the sun. Seen the world...Huh! Huh!"

Flabby face, his hair salt and pepper...Gomti looked on...

"Achchha! Say! What will be your wages? You will live on the farm—no? With the old woman?"

Gomti nodded her head.

"Give as much as you deem fair." She was quiet for a few moments, then said thoughtfully, "I will work on your farm for a whole year, for one full year! I will leave exactly a year after today. Say, will you give me rupees twenty times twenty?"

Twenty rupees, one time, make rupees twenty—this the Lala knew. Running a quick mental total he said, "Too much"

"Yes, Lala, I need just this much", Gomti said firmly.

"The full amount. Not a pie less or more."

Lala Tirpan Lal stared at her hungrily with eyes like a vulture's.

"If you will make me happy, I will give you even this much. But the work has not to suffer, understand?

"When the wild elephant comes trampling down in the night, you will have to light an instant fire and scare it away. And—and you will have to create a din too—understand?"

Gomti accepted all the conditions with her head bent.

The paddy crop was ready. The wild elephants did not come on any night, but the Lala did, regularly. A din would be created for the elephants, but when the Lala came the sobs rising in her throat had to be choked by covering the mouth with her palm. Sometimes Gomti wondered if it would not have been better if the elephants had come, after all, in place of the Lala. It would have put an end to all her sufferings.

Gomti had no idea of the sweltering heat of summer in the 'tarai'. The midday sun would spew fire, and Gomti would groan in agony from the blasts of the hot winds penetrating the thin straw with prickly heat. She would gulp down 'lotas' full of water but her thirst would remain unquenched.

Often she would be filled with longing for a glimpse of those sparkling white snow-capped peaks, visible from her front yard; the cool shade of the oak and the 'buronj', the scented breeze wafting through the pines and cedars; the gurgling, chilled water of the 'Kanthinouli'—the hill stream upon which the sun had never shone! A sip of its water could revive a dead man!

Her thirst would increase tenfold.

Wading knee-deep in mud, she would straighten the wind-blown paddy saplings. Her eternal hunger would be satiated just seeing these arm-long paddy stalks! Back in the hills, one could barely reap two or three maunds of! paddy wheat or even some coarse grain after working in the fields day and night. But here even a handful of seed, scattered carelessly, brought up a lush green crop! A man could easily be hidden amongst the tall paddy.

The humming mosquitoes would awaken Gomti in the night. Coming out into the dark courtyard, she would stand and gaze at the teak and sal; trees, standing like tall giants.

The Lala had bequeathed her a mosquito-net, for his own comfort. Plump, soft bedding too: a couple of fine sarees, but Gomti would never wear them. When the Lala scolded her, she would just wrap them around herself uncaringly. Wrapping her body in the red sarees made her feel as though she had wrapped herself in flames of fire! She felt singed from head to foot!

Come rain and there would be water everywhere, covering the fields, the bams. Standing in the murky pools, Gomti would try to piece together so many cracked images—

She would return to her mother's home, taking her husband with her. There she would labour in the fields, was it not possible to provide for three bellies? She could still work in the fields day and night without rest.

—Who knows, Pirma might be cured! She vowed to take him to the 'Dashmi' fair in Gautoda this time. The 'Dangariya" God dances there! If he would stamp? Pirma, he would be working fit and fine as before!

—They too will have a home. They would make out a piece of unclaimed fallow land somewhere in the woods, and bring it under cultivation. They would rear the goats. They would buy iron ore from the wholesale market and forge utensils.

Gomti would be lost in her world of thoughts.

"Aye Gaumti, what you are doing?" The jeep stopped before the front yard. Lala Tirpan Lal's call broke her dream.

"The crop this year is as wonderful as you are. We will weigh you in paddy this year—do you understand?"

Gomti giggled, "No use weighing me, Lala. Better weigh yourself. Surely you'll be heavier."

"I am very heavy, no? You know my load! Very heavy, no?" Lala Tirpan fixed his round cap, carefully lifting his 'dhoti', so that the murky waters should not be sprayed on it...

The Lala could not bear even the tiniest blot on his milk-white garments no matter if he was black to the core within himself!

The cool breeze blew again. The hill folk descended the peaks once again and spread out over the 'tarai' plains like swarms of locusts. The dense forests resounded with activity. The Lala was jubilant because the very first crop had been bountiful. In a fit of generosity, he had ordered five truckloads of bricks and got the labour shelter made permanent.

Gomti's wan face lit up at the sight of her relatives.

—"Khushia was looking for you."

—"Khushia searched high and low. The say he came even as far as Khatima but finding no trace, he returned with the shepherds."

—"What has come over you Gomti? You are scorched black from the heat?"

Gomti remained silent.

Later she had broken the silence and asked a relative who had come, "Did you even go to Ladhaun, ever?"

"Why not? We had all gone to Lohaghat by way of Ladhaun for a hearing in a case about the occupation of some unclaimed land. Saw Kunuva. At the very mention of your name, he burst into tears. How could have we known that you had returned to this very 'faram' (farm)? We told everyone that you might have been trampled by a wild elephant. Thy last rites have been performed. Khimu-Ka from Ladhaun performed them..."

Gomti was stunned.

"Any news from Khushal's home—?"

"They say that the elder wife slipped down the oak tree during the rains and died. The middle one is pregnant. The goat-rearing is proving profitable. He too has believed that you might have been killed by the elephant, otherwise, why would you drop behind the crowd?"

"Did you go inside our home in Ladhaun? There would hardly be any rations. They would be going around begging to pass the days..."

"Look, I will not lie to you. I did not enter the home. We were in a tearing hurry, but we did meet Pirma returning from the fields. He looked like a bird with its feathers plucked off. Tears one' s heart to pieces seeing him thus. He used to be so handsome once, like the Punjabis. That cursed Kaliya has ruined him so, woe unto him! The wretch will die begging for water. Just you see. Such wickedness? Hai! Hai!"

EIGHTEEN

Gomti had counted each day of the passing year. What had she not borne during the year-long exile? She had gone through hell, only on the strength of one hope—the day of release. "The year is over Lala. Pay my wages." Lala Tirpan Lal was merry, "What a fool you are Gomti? I am building a brick house for you, and you keep talking of returning to the hills. Who waits for you there? Say! We know that there is no one living in your family!"

"No, no Lala!" Gomti placed her fingers on the Lala's lips, "Never utter such cursed words. I had told you beforehand that I will return after working for one year, no more. Pay me for my labour. I do not ask you for more."

"Lala will raise your wages. You need not work any more. Live here and eat well, and I will look after you. Will keep you like my spouse."

"No! No!" Gomti cried, "For a whole year I was at your bidding. Say, did I ever say no to anything you asked of me? You came, brought your friends, did I ever say anything? Pay me the money Lala, or else I will hang myself at your door, do not blame me then." Gomti lowered her head on the Lala's feet.

"I bore it all for want of money Lala, otherwise, we are not of that kind...I just cannot stay on even for another day, no...I worked in your fields for one whole year. Fed on your leftovers. Tell me, what did I not do for you? Do not deter me now Lala, my life will end here. I will die without seeing my child's face..."

The Lala relented. Lifting her, he comforted her, "Alright, alright. Go if you must, 'baba'. My farm will turn to ruin, let it. I will not farm any more, what else? But you can leave."

Taking out four hundred rupees from his pocket, the Lala placed it in her palm. He handed her a little extra for the journey back home.

"Do not say to anyone that the Lala is bad. Go now..."

Gomti left behind all the fine clothes given by the Lala... did not carry a thing from him.

Discarding the 'dhoti' and 'kurti', she put on her traditional 'angdi' and 'pichhaudi'.

NINETEEN

The small tiger had lifted three lambs from the goatpen the previous night. Khushal was upset. If the tiger kept coming like this, the whole lot would be gone.

What would happen to his trade then? Pandit Budhanand was getting stricter each day, if the goats vanished, what would he do?

On his newly occupied plot of land, wheat and barley were being harvested, and he had returned from there, completely fagged out. If it rained in the night, or a hailstorm came, Khushal feared that not a single grain would reach home. That is why he was bent upon harvesting the crop and storing it as quickly as possible. Three or four men and women from the neighbourhood were coming over in shifts early the next morning to assist him. The middle one was heavy with child and could hardly move about—how would she be able to bake the 'rotis' before daybreak..."

Bolting the door he had barely fallen asleep when there was a knocking on the outer door.

For a moment he feared that it might not be the maneater pawing his door. Khushal shouted from his bed, "Arre, who is it?"

There was no reply.

The thick iron latch chain continued to rattle against the door incessantly.

Before coming out and opening the door, Khushal pried open the small window of the wooden verandah and peered in the dark.

"Hunh, la! Who is it?"

There seemed a shadow behind the door.

"I ..."

Khushal did not recognise the voice, but opened the door. Seeing the female form before him in the dark, he screamed in terror, "Who? Gomti? But you are supposed to be dead?"

Taking the shadow to be Gomti's ghost, Khushal's hair stood on end, but Gomti stood still, gazing at his face. "Yes, I had died, but I have been reborn and have come again..."

Khushal's middle wife had also come thereby then, holding the torch of a small strip of the pine bark in her right hand. In the dull light, both gazed at Gomti with terror-stricken eyes.

Gomti's skin had been scorched black by the burning heat of the sun. Her body was limp, dark shadows beneath the large, sad eyes. She could hardly be recognised.

This could not be Gomti—it must be her ghost.

Both tried to push her out with trembling hands and bolt the doors—

"Go, ye! Why have you returned after dying? It was heard that your last rites were performed by Khimua Lwar[42] the 'pind-daan'[43] done...!"

---

42. 'Lwar' - Ironsmith

43. 'Pind-daan' - Ritual bidding farewell to the departed soul

"Should you not have performed my last rites? Were you not my husband?" Gomti was suddenly overcome with rage. She stared at them, gnashing her teeth. Both of them shrank back in fear and took shelter behind the door.

"My soul has been saved, but what about yours? That is why I have come. Had you not prevented me from going to meet my son, without first making good the compensation amount? Here, count these! Twenty times twenty in all!" Gomti took out the knotted rag from the pocket of her 'angdi' and slapped the rupees on Khushal's face,

"Take these and count them! The full amount? Now am I free of you? Fear not, I shall never cross your threshold again...!" Gomti vanished in the dark, just as swiftly as she had come.

TWENTY

The sun was rising as Gomti, crossing the villages of Phadka and Manar, climbed the rise of the village Ladhaun, taking the path alongside the river. Panting with the effort, as she went up, the menfolk of the village came into view. Their heads shaved and faces mournful, they seemed to be returning after a dip in the river Josyuda.

Seeing Gomti, long since given up as dead, they were dumb-founded with fear.

"You had died! Your last rites were performed! From where have you come now?" someone asked, trembling like a leaf.

"For you people. I was dead even while living..."

Gomti choked over her tears, "Who would have done this penance had I died...?"

Shaven-headed Khimu-Ka looked shorter still. Taking Gomti aside, he said in a broken voice, "Our Pirma died last night, daughter-in-law! Had you returned a day earlier, perhaps this would not have happened..."

Gomti stood paralysed, dumb with shock. Not a sob. not a sound, not a word escaped her lips.

Khimu-Ka led her home by the hand, she followed him lifelessly—like a clay statue!

"The hut caught fire last night and the unfortunate one perished in it!" an old gentleman standing nearby, said sadly. Yes, the straw hut had been gutted, black poles, some half-burnt, some reduced to cinders, lay sprawled haphazardly on the ground singed black by the fire. The old rags, the broken wooden box, the uniform belt that Devram had forgotten to take along—all were reduced to ashes. The half-burnt rag that had been Pirma's torn shirt, fluttered from the peg.

"Ija, you are back?" Kunnu leapt towards her and she gathered him in her arms.

"All of them killed Bajyu yesterday, Ija! Where had you gone, leaving us behind?" Kunnu shook with sobs.

Khimu-Ka's old wife took Gomti to her home.

Then, taking her aside, she whispered furtively. "Swear by God that you will not say anything to anyone, daughter-in-law! Otherwise, these demons will bury us alive."

Taking her mouth to Gomti's ear, she confided in hushed tones, "These people murdered our Pirma. He had taken the cattle to the pasture yesterday. While returning from there, Kaliya's bull slipped into a ditch and broke a leg, God knows how! Kaliya dashed out in rage, and no one knows what overcame him. In the darkness, he dealt such a blow on Pirma's head with his 'lathi' that the poor lad fell dead. Did not even ask for water, poor soul!"

"..."

"Realizing what he had done, Kaliya trembled in panic. He roamed till midnight, cornering the village elders into a meeting in his house. There would be hell to pay, should the police and the 'patwari' get wind of his crime. The whole village would be devastated—manslaughter was no light matter. Pirma's corpse was tied up quietly, doused with kerosene and ignited by Kaliya.

All were told that the hut had caught fire and the poor boy had perished in it...the heartless brutes are responsible for such a gruesome deed. Tejuva had suggested flinging even Kunnua into the flames, but he was destined to live. After his father's death, the poor child ran away, God knows where! O Goddess Bhagwati ... mother..."

Khimu-Ka's wife folded her hands, "You saved this child's life..."

Gomti seemed turned into stone. Wide-eyed with shock she gazed on—crazed.

Remaining thus for a few moments she suddenly came to life. None knew what flashed across her mind. Clutching Kunnu's hand she ran like a woman insane. Halting for a moment in Kaliya-Ka's front yard she cursed, "Kaliya murderer, you burnt my Kunuva's father! If I do not roast you alive the same way...I...I am...I am not a true woman."

Gnashing her teeth, Gomti fled to the woods, her hair flying, her clothes dishevelled, but she seemed unaware of it all. She ran on like a woman possessed.

It was a desolate evening. Night fell, but none in the village lighted the kitchen fire. All were in mourning for Pirma, none would eat.

Sleep overcame them.

The third lap of the dark, dark night was not over yet, when suddenly, the people of the surrounding villages woke suddenly to see tongues of flame leap up to the sky, far away in the enveloping darkness. The strew hutments of a village burnt like pyres, and were soon reduced to ashes.

Holding the hand of her child, a mother looking like the reincarnation of 'Kaal Bhairavi'[44] was seen walking away from the settlement,...going, God knew where...? Dawn was yet to be.

44. 'Kaal Bhairavi' - The goddess of annihilation

www.ingramcontent.com/pod-product-compliance
Ingram Content Group UK Ltd.
Pitfield, Milton Keynes, MK11 3LW, UK
UKHW042015190726
13854UKWH00005B/2298